SLEEPING ANGEL

by

Greg Herren

A Division of Bold Strokes Books

2011

SLEEPING ANGEL

ISBN 10: 1-60282-214-X
ISBN 13: 978-1-60282-214-6

This Trade Paperback Original Is Published By
Bold Strokes Books, Inc.
P.O. Box 249
Valley Falls, NY 12185

First Edition: March 2011

CREDITS
Editor: Stacia Seaman
Production Design: Stacia Seaman
Cover Design by Sheri (graphicartist2020@hotmail.com)

Dedication

This is for Stan and Janet Duval, with deepest gratitude for the LSU–Ole Miss tickets. GEAUX TIGERS!

PROLOGUE

He was driving too fast, and knew he should ease his foot off the gas pedal, bringing the car down to a safer, more manageable speed.

But he couldn't bring himself to do it.

"Hang in there, buddy," he muttered grimly under his breath, taking his eyes off the road for just a moment to glance in the rearview mirror into the backseat. What he saw wasn't encouraging. Sean's eyes were closed, and he couldn't tell if Sean was still breathing.

The blood—there was so much of it, and it was everywhere.

He swallowed and took a deep breath, trying to hold down the panic. He had to stay calm. He couldn't let the fear take over, he just couldn't. He had to hold himself together. He had to get into town, to get Sean to the hospital before it was too late—if it wasn't already too late.

Don't think like that, he scolded himself, *everything's going to be okay. You just have to get to the hospital. Hold it together until you get there, okay? You can do it.*

Once he was there and the emergency room staff had taken over—*then*, and only then, would he be able to let go.

He still couldn't believe what happened, *was* happening. It didn't seem real. His mind was having trouble wrapping itself around it all, accepting it as reality. It was like some horrible nightmare he couldn't wake up from no matter how hard he tried. A bead of sweat ran down his face.

But it was real—all too real.

It had happened so fast. One minute everything was fine, and the next the entire world had gone crazy.

He still couldn't believe it.

But the proof was in the backseat.

Focus on the road. You're not too far from town.

His ears were still ringing. He could still smell burnt powder in his nose. The whole scene kept replaying itself over and over again in his mind, like some horrible movie on an endless loop. He forced the images out of his mind before the panic could start to well up inside him again. He was already a little numb— *shock, I must be in shock*—but he'd reacted quickly, without even thinking twice. He'd picked Sean up and run with him to the car, put him in the backseat, and driven off. He couldn't get a signal with his cell phone out at the Ledge—which was why it was such a popular hangout for teenagers. There was no way to call for help—so the only thing to do was go get help, and he couldn't just leave Sean out there to die alone. No, he had to get him to the hospital. That was all that mattered for now—getting Sean help, saving his life. Everything else could wait.

There would be time to think later, to piece together what had happened out there at the Ledge and figure out why.

He just had to get to the hospital as fast as he could.

He pressed down harder on the gas pedal. The old Honda protested—it had never been much good for climbing inclines— and he cursed under his breath. "Come on, come on, come on," he muttered, willing the car to go faster, to make it up the incline.

The car whined but kept climbing and he tried to remember. Was this the last incline before town?

The little car reached the top and he blew out a sigh of relief as it picked up speed. There was a long flat stretch for a while, he remembered, and there was only one more climb before hitting the city limits. And the hospital was only a few blocks into town.

The drive had never seemed to take this long before—and he was going a lot faster than he usually did. He glanced in the rearview mirror. Sean's eyes were open, his mouth moving, but no sound was coming out.

"Don't try to talk, buddy," he called back over his shoulder. "Save your strength. We're almost there, hang in there, buddy, okay? Everything's going to be all right."

I can hold it together till we get to the hospital, he reminded himself.

After that, he would do whatever needed to be done. Talk to the police, go back out to the Ledge, do whatever was necessary to make this right. But the hospital had to come first. That was all that mattered. He had to get Sean help—and then he could collapse, cry, have a breakdown, whatever it was his body needed to cope with what he'd witnessed, the horror that happened out at the Ledge.

He would never forget it.

The crack of the gunshot, the look on Sean's face as the blood spurted out from his chest and his body fell backward. The blood, so much blood, and that horrible gurgling sound coming from Sean's throat—

He pushed those thoughts out of his mind. *Later, there's time for that later. Stay focused, pay attention to the road, get him to the hospital.*

He swallowed and gripped the steering wheel even tighter, his knuckles turning white.

He'd never driven this fast out on the county road. His mother would scream at him if she saw the speedometer, saw how fast the old battered green Honda Accord was going on the winding road. Other kids might be daredevils, other kids might get their cars up to ninety on this road, but he never had. He could hear his father's voice, lecturing: *Your car isn't a toy—it's a responsibility. It would be one thing if you killed yourself by being reckless at the wheel—but what if you killed someone else? You're responsible for everyone's life riding in that car with you, and you're responsible for the lives of everyone else on the road. Driving is a responsibility, Eric. Driving a car is not like playing a video game, son. A car is a killing machine if it's not respected. Thousands of people are killed or maimed because of careless drivers every year.*

And he'd always taken responsibility seriously—whether it was driving, taking care of his little brother, babysitting for the Baxter kids next door. "You're so responsible, Eric," Mrs. Baxter would always say as she gave him a twenty from her purse. "I never worry about the kids for a minute when you're here."

But this was a bigger responsibility than he'd ever been given before. Sean's life was in his hands. He could die—was dying—and Eric had to get him help, get him to the hospital.

He couldn't fail.

He couldn't let Sean die.

It's not your fault. You couldn't have known this would happen. There was nothing you could have done to stop it from happening.

There was a gurgling sound from the backseat, and it didn't sound good. It wasn't normal, and he felt the panic rise again. "Hang in there!" he shouted. "We'll be there before you know it!" He took his eyes off the road to look in the rearview mirror. Sean had sunk down in the seat. The blood—

It was everywhere. Sean's shirt was soaked through with it. His hand, pressed to the wound, was coated with it. But he could see Sean's chest moving up and down. He was still breathing, that was something, he was still alive and it wouldn't take much longer…it couldn't be much longer.

Please, he added in his head. He was gripping the steering wheel so tightly his hands were starting to ache and cramp a little bit. *Please hold on. Please make it to the hospital. Please.*

It was too much responsibility. Another person's life was too much.

Another drop of sweat ran down from his scalp and along the right side of his face. He took his right hand off the wheel to wipe it off.

Everything had changed in just a few minutes. One minute, he was his old self, not a care in the world. When he woke up that morning, it had seemed like it was going to be a great day. He'd felt like himself for the first time since—*don't think about that*, he reminded himself. But as he got out of bed, he knew everything was going to be all right. He *knew* it somehow. He was whistling as he went downstairs for breakfast. He had mowed the lawn, cleaned his room, and done some other chores for his mom while she was off running errands. He'd showered and changed—and made the decision to fool around online before heading to the weight room.

If only he hadn't checked his e-mail. If only he hadn't checked his Facebook page until later, after lifting weights. It would have been too late then and he wouldn't have gotten involved. Things would have changed—there was no doubt of that, but he wouldn't have been right in the middle of it.

He almost hadn't gone out to the Ledge. He hadn't wanted to go, he didn't owe Sean anything—why waste his time meeting him? What could Sean possibly have to say to him that would make the least amount of difference? Besides, going all the way out there was going to have him pressed for time. He was supposed to be at the weight room at one. Coach Roberts didn't like his players to be late. He was already in dutch with Coach Roberts as it was—he'd skipped a few days. He'd gone back and forth, debating with himself, finally deciding to go out and see what Sean wanted, hear what he had to say. He'd driven out there, listening to the college radio station, singing along with Coldplay. It was a beautiful summer day, the sun was out and it wasn't humid—he was in a good mood for the first time in days.

And less than fifteen minutes after he arrived at the Ledge, the gun roared and Sean went down, his life pumping out through his fingers.

Nothing was ever going to be the same again.

Don't think about it. It doesn't matter right now. There'll be plenty of time to think about it later.

If only I hadn't checked my Facebook page.

He wouldn't have been there to hear the gunshot.

He wouldn't have been there to see the surprise on Sean's face.

He wouldn't have been there to see Sean fall backward, blood already spurting from the wound, his hands moving in slow motion to where the bullet had entered his body.

He wouldn't have gotten blood spattered on him.

Eric was covered in blood. It was all over him. His Woodbridge High Wildcats T-shirt was soaked in it, and it was getting sticky and tacky as it dried. He could see it on his arms and his bare legs, and for a moment he felt like he was going to throw up, but he fought it down.

After I get to the hospital I can be sick. After the hospital I can be afraid, give in to the panic. But right now I have to get him there. If I can get him there they might be able to save him. It's up to me. He'll die if I don't get there.

It was too much responsibility.

But he didn't have a choice. It was up to him.

The speedometer crept past seventy.

He thought about easing up on the gas pedal; it was a natural reflex, one he'd trained himself to have. He didn't like to speed. *The faster you go, the less control you have over the car,* he heard his father saying. *The faster you go, the less the car weighs, the less pull gravity has on it. If you're going thirty miles an hour and you start to lose control, it's much easier to get it back than if you're going forty.*

There was a sharp turn coming. He could see the warning sign coming up on the right. Fifty miles per hour was the speed limit for negotiating the turn safely. He took his foot off the gas pedal. *What are you doing, you've been with other drivers when they've taken this curve going much faster than fifty and they didn't lose control, they stayed on the road, and if you're ever going to take this curve at faster than fifty now is the time, he's dying back there in the backseat, and you've got to get him to the hospital.*

He swallowed and put his foot back down on the gas pedal.

The speedometer, which had dropped back in the direction of sixty, started creeping back the other way.

Don't be afraid, you can do it. Others have, you know it.

The Accord flew past the sign and he saw the turn coming up. It wasn't quite ninety degrees—it wasn't that sharp but it was a tight one, and in front of the road he could see trees and the drop off, the sheer drop-off the side of the mountain.

He bit his lip and said a silent prayer.

He started to turn the wheel as he eased up on the gas pedal, just a little bit. There was a guardrail but he knew it wouldn't stop the car if he went off the road, the little Accord would blast right through it like it was tin foil and shoot off the side of the mountain and it wouldn't matter anymore.

But the tires gripped the road as he went into the turn. The driver's side went up a bit, but the tires didn't leave the pavement.

He started to let out a sigh of relief, started to relax, when he heard a loud bang.

He barely had time to think *what was that* when the front of the car veered to the right and crashed into the guardrail, which didn't hold, didn't slow the car at all, just crumpled as sparks flew up from the collision of metal on metal.

And then the guardrail was gone and all he saw were the trees in front of him.

The car sailed into the air and came down nose first, and there was a deafening crash.

The windshield snaked with cracks and shattered as the air bag inflated with a loud bang, throwing him back into his seat.

As the car flipped over, chemicals blew out of a vent in the side of the air bag. The acrid smell made his nose burn and his eyes water.

There was another crash as the back end of the car smashed into the ground and he could hear the metal crumpling.

I hope there's nothing important in the trunk, he thought crazily as the car continued its crashing descent down the side of the mountain, as windows shattered and he jerked from side to side, banging his head on the door and then on the roof of the car, and it was all happening so fast but it somehow seemed to be happening in slow motion, and still the car kept falling and rolling over and over even as his air bag deflated.

He heard someone screaming.

His head started hurting and there was pain in his legs and in one of his arms, there was blinding pain everywhere, everything hurt, and still the car kept moving, an endless nightmare, over and over again, and more things hurt, there was more pain and then he wasn't really aware of anything, except the pain.

The car came to a rest, the engine ticking.

His ears rang as blood ran down into his eyes. He was in pain, he hurt, oh God, how bad it hurt.

He closed his eyes.

And felt himself drifting.

He couldn't open his eyes.

But he felt calm.

The stress, the panic, the pain—all of it was gone.

There was nothing but a bright light—and it was warm and inviting.

He moved toward it.

Nothing matters anymore.

Chapter One

He was floating.

Everything was gray as he drifted weightless through what sometimes seemed like clouds—other times it seemed like the morning mist in the spring. There was no sound, no color, no sensory stimulation of any kind. He just drifted, not feeling anything, with no sense of time or place. The gray began to brighten and he winced away from the growing of the light. The gray lightened, changing to a vibrant red. He heard shuffling footsteps from what seemed like miles away. Every so often there was a beep, and as it entered his awareness he noticed the beep actually came at regular intervals. There was mumbling noise, sounds coming from human throats, but he couldn't understand what words they were saying. It was just noise but he knew it *had* to be words, had to mean something, because humans didn't make noise just to make noise—and there were answering noises in a different tone and register. *What are they saying, what are they talking about?* flashed through his mind and he strained through the fog, trying to recognize and interpret the sounds as words. It bothered him that he couldn't understand because he *should* understand, and as he strained to listen harder, he became aware of a dull throbbing. First it was in his head—a dull ache that seemed to hurt more each time it pulsed, and there was pain somewhere else—*my ribs, it's my ribs*—then it got stronger, the pain was horrible as the sounds faded away all he was aware of was the pain. It wouldn't stop. It just kept getting stronger and stronger. It was too much—then it started fading away again. The reddish light changed as the pain faded until everything was gray again.

He was floating again through gray mist. It was all he was aware of, that safe place in the mist where nothing hurt, where time and space had no meaning, and it was peaceful, oh so peaceful as he drifted. Nothing mattered as long as he kept floating.

The gray began to change to red again. He wasn't drifting anymore. He was lying down and everything was red. Other things began to creep into his consciousness—that regular beeping, shuffling sounds and murmuring voices, too low or too far away for him to understand what was being said. He resisted. He didn't want to leave the mist again. The last time there'd been pain, he remembered that—it started as a dull throbbing and got stronger until he couldn't stand it anymore. He didn't want to hurt. He just wanted to be at peace and keep floating.

He felt something warm cover his hand. It was warm and a little damp and it applied pressure on his hand.

Someone is squeezing my hand.

He tried to identify the noises, focused and concentrated on the mumbling sound.

"…it's a miracle he is still alive…"

"We've all been praying." His hand was squeezed again. "Everyone loves Eric." The voice broke, choked with a sob. "I know he's going to wake up—and I'm going to be here when it happens. I don't want him to wake up and be alone."

He tried to open his eyes but they wouldn't obey. He concentrated, focusing all of his energy, but they refused to open. The sounds were very clear. He heard shoes shuffling around him. Something soft and warm touched his forehead. "I'm sure he will, Mrs. Matthews."

"Please call me Melanie."

"He sure has a lot of friends." He heard the shuffling noise again. "I don't think I've ever seen a hospital room so full of flowers before."

Hospital? I'm in the hospital? Why? What's wrong with me?

He focused on opening his eyes again. They wouldn't open.

The throbbing started again. It got worse, so bad he could hardly stand it—

"He's moaning! He's in pain!" The hand let go of his.

Everything else faded. He was only aware of the pain.

There was some shuffling, some clanking noises he was barely aware of, the pain was so intense he couldn't notice anything else it hurt so bad his *head* felt like it was going to explode—

Everything faded again to gray and he was floating.

Sounds again echoed through the gray. Someone was talking.

The voice was female.

"...I don't know if you can hear me, but everyone's praying for you, everyone wants you to wake up and walk out of this hospital..."

He willed his eyes to open.

This time, they obeyed.

It was bright—too bright and too many colors, reds and yellows and greens and blues and spots danced in front of his eyes and he squeezed them shut again. The colors and the light hurt.

"I think he opened his eyes for a second! Did you see that?"

"Let me ring for the doctor."

He smelled bleach, and ammonia, and flowers.

"Eric, can you hear me? It's Mom, son." His hand was squeezed again.

Eric? That must be my name, that must be who I am.

He tried to answer but his lips were dry, his throat ached and no sound came out.

"He's trying to talk! Latrice, did you see that?"

His hand was squeezed even tighter. He willed his eyes open and found himself looking at a woman. She looked haggard. Her short brown hair was in disarray; there were dark circles under her eyes, lines at the corners of her mouth. Her blue eyes blinked and tears started flowing from them. She leaned in closer to him. He could smell her breath—stale coffee and peppermints. "Eric, honey, can you hear me?"

"Yes," he managed to say. It hurt his throat, and his voice sounded unused, rusty. "Thirsty," he croaked out.

The woman wiped at her eyes. "Everything's going to be all right, Eric. I promise you."

"All…right…" he managed to get out before the effort exhausted him. His eyes closed. Red turned to gray and he floated again.

But this time was different than the other times. The beeping intruded, and there were flashes of light and color. Images floated along with him in the gray fog—images of the woman who held his hand, images of a woman in green scrubs checking monitors and the bag attached to the needle stuck in his arm, and thirst—always the thirst was there. And when the gray turned to red again and he opened his eyes, the woman in green scrubs smiled down at him. She was doing something to the needle in his arm, and he croaked out the word *thirsty* again.

She slipped a chip of ice between his lips, and the cold

wetness soothed the dryness inside his mouth. "How are you feeling?" she asked, picking up a cloth and wiping at his forehead. "You gave us a scare."

She was pretty, he decided, even though she looked really tired. Her big brown eyes were full of concern, and her smile didn't quite reach them.

He swallowed. "Hospital?" He managed to say, and as the word came out, a rush of images rushed through his mind. He saw the front of the hospital, with the driveway and the parking lot, the cement letters spelling out Woodbridge General Hospital across the lip of the overhanging ledge over the front doors. He turned his eyes away from her. Everywhere he looked there were flowers, in vases and on every available surface. Roses and daisies and mums and balloons shaped like hearts with *Get Well Soon* written across them, cards and stuffed animals, bears and... *dogs*, the word came to him—and the curtains were closed. The room was painted beige, and he could smell bleach and ammonia. *Nurse, she's a nurse.*

"How...long?" His voice didn't sound right to him, and he moved his lips again. His throat ached. She slid another piece of ice through his lips, and smiled down at him.

"Just relax, Eric," she cooed at him. "Don't strain yourself, okay? I rang for the doctor, he'll be here in a minute, okay?" She held up one of her hands, making a fist. Her index finger uncurled. "How many fingers am I holding up?"

"One." He said it without having to think. The mist was fading. "What happened? Why am I here?"

"You were in an accident," she replied, "but we've been taking really good care of you."

He was tired, so very tired, and when he closed his eyes everything went gray again. And he floated.

"...he was awake and lucid. He knew I was holding up one

finger. He wanted to know what happened, how long he'd been here…"

He opened his eyes. The nurse was talking to a man in green scrubs. The man was young, with stubble all over his chin and cheeks. He, too, looked tired. A mop of curly dark hair perched on top of his round head. He was holding a metal folder in his hands, looking at the inside and making notes with a pen. The man looked at him. "Eric." He smiled and moved closer, alongside the bed. He shined a light into Eric's eyes. "How you feeling, buddy?"

"Okay." He tried to move but couldn't. Everything seemed kind of fuzzy. "I…can't…move…"

"We have you on some serious pain medication," the man replied. "If you could move, you'd be a medical miracle." He moved to the bottom of the bed, and Eric felt something being lifted off his feet, and then something tickling the bottoms.

"Tickles," Eric said. "Stop…please."

The man laughed, and Eric felt something on the inside of his legs. "Can you feel that?"

"Yes." Eric replied, wrinkling his forehead. "How… long…"

"Have you been here?" The man made some more notes inside the metal folder, closed it, and hung it from the end of the bed. "It's been a little over two weeks, Eric." He moved back alongside the bed until he was right next to Eric. "You've been sleeping for almost fifteen days."

"Why…what…" The words were so hard to get out. His tongue felt like it was fighting him. He closed his eyes and concentrated. "Accident?"

"Yes, you were in a car accident," the man replied, watching Eric's face. "Do you remember anything about it?"

Eric opened his eyes. The man looked so nice, like he wanted to help him. He took a deep breath and searched his mind. There was nothing there.

Nothing.

He didn't remember anything.

He felt panic trying to rise, but his mind was fuzzy. Everything was fuzzy, and everything was going gray. "I... don't...remember..." He closed his eyes and floated off into the gray again.

He opened his eyes. The room was dark, except for a small light. He turned his eyes in that direction. It wasn't much of a light, a narrow, long sliver being directed at something the woman in the chair next to his bed was holding open. *It's a book*, he thought, focusing on the spine. *What the Dead Know* by Laura Lippman, he read. She was close to the end. She was looking through a pair of wire-rimmed glasses and frowning. Her eyes moved back and forth and her lips moved slightly as she read. She turned a page, unaware he was watching her. He remembered seeing her before—she was the one who said she was his mother. She was wearing a pair of shorts and a T-shirt with a picture of a cat on it, and her feet were perched on the side of the bed.

His mind was clearer, he realized, there wasn't any fuzziness or strangeness. The gray mist was gone. He tried licking his dried lips but his tongue was dry. "Thirsty" was all he managed to croak out.

The book dropped from her hands and the thin light shone right into his eyes for a moment before it moved again, leaving dancing red lights in his vision. "Eric? Are you awake?" The woman's lower lip was trembling, and she was grabbing something, pushing down with her finger. She moved in closer. "Honey, oh, thank God, you're awake! Can I get you something?"

"Thirsty?" He closed his eyes and concentrated. She was

his mother—he remembered her saying it before. But he didn't recognize her. He searched through his mind. There was nothing there. He opened his eyes again as she put a piece of ice into his mouth.

"Oh, thank God." She wiped at her eyes. "Everything's going to be okay, honey."

He heard the sound of the door opening and he slowly turned his head. There was a nurse—not the same one as before, this one was black—walking over to the bed, smiling at him, checking machines around his bed. *That's where the beeping is coming from*, he thought as she pressed her fingers to his wrist and looked at her watch. She got the metal folder from the bottom of the bed and made notes in it. She looked up and caught him watching her. She smiled at him as she hooked the folder back on the bottom of the bed. "Hi, Eric. I'm Latrice, your night nurse." She walked around the left side of the bed. "How you feeling tonight?"

He tried to smile at her and felt the corners of his mouth lift a bit. "I…feel…okay."

"You're healing pretty well." Nurse Latrice smiled at him. "But you were a pretty big mess when we brought you in. We were worried about you."

"Accident?"

"Yes, you were in an accident," the other woman—*Mom*—said. "Your car went off the road. Don't you remember?"

He rolled his head on the pillow till he was looking at her. He closed his eyes and thought. There was nothing. "No."

"It's okay," Nurse Latrice said from his other side. "It's not unusual in cases of trauma that you don't remember what happened."

Mom leaned over and kissed his forehead. "Don't you worry about a thing, son. You just lie there and rest, okay?"

I don't remember who you are, he thought. *You're my mother and I don't know you.*

"I…don't…remember," he said again, closing his eyes. *What's wrong with me? I don't remember anything.*

Everything was gone. When he tried to think, all he saw was gray fog.

There was nothing.

His memory was all gray. "I don't remember *anything*."

His eyes filled with tears of frustration. There had to be something he could remember.

"Anything?" Mom asked. Her voice was hesitant, fearful. She was biting her lower lip, clenching her fists. She smiled, but it looked forced. "You remember me, don't you, Eric?"

He closed his eyes again.

"Eric?"

Everything went gray again. But this time, there were images floating with him through the mist—images that made no sense to him. He saw Nurse Latrice walking into an apartment, kicking off her shoes and sighing as she collapsed on a threadbare couch, reaching for a remote control and turning on a television set. She hobbled tiredly into a kitchen, opened the refrigerator and got a can of diet soda, popping the top and weaving back to the couch. She lit a cigarette and took a long steady inhale, blowing the smoke toward the ceiling as she curled her legs underneath her and flipped through the channels. Her eyelids started to droop, her head nodding until finally it just dropped forward. The lit cigarette fell from her hand into the carpet, which started smoldering.

He opened his eyes.

He was alone in the room.

He shivered and pressed the little button on the plastic box. There was light coming from the other side of the curtains now.

Another woman, one he'd never seen before, walked into his room wearing green scrubs. "Do you need something?"

"Nurse Latrice—"

"I'm sorry, honey, she went off duty two hours ago."

"She's falling asleep with a cigarette in her hand." His voice sounded strange to him, but he kept talking. "She's going to set her apartment on fire."

"Honey, you just had a bad dream—"

"Please call her," he whispered, "and call the fire department."

"It was just a bad dream, Eric." She smiled at him. "Just close your eyes and go back to sleep."

"Please?"

She sighed, pulling a cell phone out of her pocket. "If you promise to go back to sleep?" He nodded, and she punched a few buttons. She winked at him. "Hi, Latrice, this is Charlotte—I'm sorry to bother you but—" Her eyes widened and she stared at him. "Of course, oh my God, of course, call me back as soon as you can. Are you all right?" She closed her phone, her face draining of color. "She's waiting for the fire department," she whispered. "Her apartment caught fire..." She took a few steps away from him. "How—*how* did you know that?" she whispered. She looked frightened as she kept backing away.

His eyelids felt heavy. He could barely keep them open. "As long as she's okay," he whispered. He closed his eyes and everything went gray again.

And he was floating again. Voices swam in and out of his consciousness, whispering voices.

"He *knew* her apartment was on fire."

"That isn't possible."

"I'm telling you he knew! He told me to call her!"

He floated in the gray mist, slightly aware of sounds and movement around his bed. Several times he tried to open his eyes, to talk, to respond to what he was hearing. But the mist wouldn't release him. It was so peaceful and tranquil and he couldn't fight it, didn't really want to.

The mist started to fade again. There were hushed voices— angry voices arguing. He could barely make out what they were saying. He swam up through the grayness, and his awareness grew stronger. He could smell flowers, antiseptic, bleach. The muffled sounds became clearer as the mist cleared.

"...I'm telling you he doesn't remember the accident! Why don't you believe me?"

He didn't open his eyes. He recognized the voice—the woman who said she was Mom.

"Maybe he remembers now," a male voice replied. "I have to question him, Melanie. We've been waiting over two weeks to talk to him."

"He almost died!" she replied angrily. "And now he's barely been conscious for what? A little less than twenty-four hours? You've had to wait all this time, what would it hurt to wait another day?"

"Melanie—" the male voice pleaded. "The sooner we clear this up, the better. That Brody boy was shot, and he was in Eric's car. There's already talk I'm protecting him. The Brodys want answers—they *deserve* answers, Melanie. What if the situation was reversed? Put yourself in their place. They lost their son!"

"And I almost lost mine!"

"But the sooner we know what happened—"

The Brody boy? Shot? And in my car? How is that possible? Why can't I remember that?

He tried.

He searched his memory.

There was nothing there, other than the gray mist.

He opened his eyes. They were standing over by the door. Mom's back was to Eric, and the man in the blue uniform saw his eyes were open. He stepped around Mom and headed over to the bed.

"Arnie—" Mom pleaded.

Arnie sat down in the chair next to the bed. He was balding, with what hair he had left a salt-and-pepper mix. There was gray in the dark mustache under his crooked nose. The gold nameplate over his right shirt pocket said *A. Rolnik*. "Hey, Eric, how are you?" he asked in a soft voice. "You mind talking to me?"

"Who—" Eric licked his dry lips. "Who is the Brody kid?"

"Sean Brody, Eric." Arnie Rolnik glanced over at Mom, whose eyes had widened. "Eric, your mother says you don't remember the accident. Can you try to remember? It's important."

He searched his memory again. He focused, concentrated. There was nothing but the mist. He shook his head. "I can't remember anything." He dry swallowed. He could feel panic rising, his breath was coming faster. "What happened? Please tell me."

"You don't know why Sean Brody was in your car?"

Eric closed his eyes. He shook his head. Tears of frustration formed in his eyes. "I don't know who that *is*." His voice was shaking. "Tell me who he is! Tell me what happened! I don't remember."

"It's okay, honey, don't get upset," Mom said, giving Arnie a dirty look. She crossed over to the bed and took his hand. "You've known Sean since you were a little boy, Eric. Remember? He used to come over to our house all the time. You used to play with him, remember?"

"I don't remember," Eric repeated. "Why can't I remember?" He squeezed her hand.

"Shh, honey." She glared at Arnie over the bed. "You're upsetting him. This can wait, Arnie."

"What's wrong with me?" Eric demanded. He choked back a sob. "Why can't I remember anything?" He closed his eyes. He took a deep breath and concentrated. "There's nothing there— just the mist."

"Eric," Arnie said. "Look at me." Eric turned his head so he was looking at him. Arnie peered into Eric's eyes. "Do you know who I am, Eric?"

Eric shook his head. "She calls you Arnie." His lower lip trembled. "Should I know you?"

Mom gasped, her hand going up to her mouth.

"Are you sure, Eric?" Arnie said softly. "You don't recognize me?"

Eric shook his head.

"I'm your uncle." Arnie straightened up, looking at Mom. His face was grim. "Melanie, we need to get the doctor in here."

"Eric, honey," Mom said. "Look at me." She took a deep breath. "You know who I am, don't you?"

A tear rolled out of his eye. "You—you're my mother, aren't you?"

"Yes. But don't you know that?"

Eric shook his head. "No." He couldn't help it. He started crying. He started shaking. "Why can't I remember anything?" he choked out.

"I'll get Dr. Weston," Arnie said. He gave Mom a look and hurried out of the room.

Mom sat down on the side of the bed. "Shh, baby, don't cry, baby," she soothed, her voice shaking. "It's going to be okay, you'll see, just stay calm."

He nodded, wiping at his face. "I don't—there's nothing there," he said. "Nothing, I don't—I can't—" He turned his head away from her.

He closed his eyes and tried again.

He searched through his mind, trying to find anything, any memory at all.

"Relax, baby," she crooned to him, stroking his forehead. "You don't worry about a thing, okay?"

"What happened to Sean?" he asked, afraid to open his eyes. "I heard you two talking. Somebody shot him?"

"Forget about it for now. It isn't important—you just need to rest, okay?" She squeezed his hand.

Relax. He couldn't. He couldn't remember anything—but he couldn't forget the words Arnie had said when they both thought he was still asleep.

Sean Brody was shot and was in his car, Melanie.

"He's dead, isn't he?"

"Eric—"

"Tell me the truth." He clenched his hands. "I want to know the truth." He opened his eyes and glared at her.

She bit her lower lip and nodded. "Yes, Eric." She swallowed. "He's dead. He was shot. The police found his body in your car when they found you. They say"—her voice broke—"the accident—they think he was already dead when the car crashed."

Oh, God. "They think I killed him?" *Why can't I remember? Oh, God, could I have* killed *someone?*

"Nobody thinks that," she said urgently. "Nobody. Shhh, just relax, okay? Your uncle's getting the doctor—"

"Did I kill him?" he whispered.

"Don't say that. Don't ever say that, do you understand

me?" She looked stricken. "It isn't possible. You would never do anything like that, understand?" She wiped at her eyes. "Don't ever let me hear you saying anything like that ever again, is that clear?"

"But—"

"No." She shook her head, her lips set in a grim line. "You didn't shoot him, Eric. You couldn't have. I won't hear of it."

Eric closed his eyes. *I have to remember.*

Did I kill Sean?

CHAPTER TWO

S o, how's our patient today?" Dr. Weston breezed into Eric's room sporting a huge friendly smile. He picked up Eric's chart from the end of the bed and flipped through it for a few moments. "Are you feeling any pain?"

"No," Eric replied. "I mean, I feel *weird*, but I don't hurt anywhere."

"Glad to hear there's no pain." He made a note and hung the chart back up. He pulled out a penlight and shone it into Eric's eyes. He smiled, turning the penlight off and putting it back in his pocket. "What do you mean by weird?"

Eric bit his lower lip and shook his head. "I don't understand," he said, trying to keep his voice from shaking. "What's happened to me?"

Dr. Weston sat down on the side of Eric's bed. He was wearing blue scrubs with a white lab coat over them. He looked to be in his early fifties, with dark brown eyes and gray streaks in his dark hair. "Well, you know you were in an accident," he said, "and you got a nasty concussion—along with some bruised ribs, a sprained ankle, and a broken arm—all of which are healing nicely." Dr. Weston patted his hand. "Apparently, you also got amnesia."

"Will I get my memories back?"

Dr. Weston hesitated for a moment. "It's likely, Eric. But there's also a chance you won't." He cleared his throat. "You have what's called *trauma-induced retrograde amnesia*, which pretty much is what it sounds like. It was induced by the trauma to your head in the accident, and *retrograde* means you lost all of your memories. In some cases, the memory loss can be permanent." He shook his head. "But in most cases, it isn't. Sometimes the memories come back gradually, sometimes a trigger can bring them all back at once." He shrugged. "I can't promise you you'll get your memory back, but I would say it's highly likely." He looked at the laptop sitting on the nightstand. "Do you remember how to use your laptop?"

Eric nodded. His mother had his father bring it by while they waited for Dr. Weston to stop in. She'd left to get some coffee.

The brief visit with his father had been awkward and uncomfortable. His father was a total stranger. He knew, somehow, he was supposed to *feel* something when he looked at his father, but there was nothing—just like with his mother. After a few moments his father—*Dad*—had made excuses and left.

Mom kept trying to get him to remember things—bringing up things from their shared past, and her disappointment when he didn't remember was getting harder and harder for him to handle. As soon as she'd left to get coffee he'd turned the laptop on, and even remembered how to connect to the hospital's wireless service. It was automatic—he didn't even have to think. He knew that the lowercase blue *e* was Internet Explorer. But when he looked at the bookmarks bar, none of the websites sounded in the least bit familiar. He pulled up Facebook—but didn't remember his password or what his e-mail address was in order to sign in. He finally closed it and put it back on the nightstand. "I don't remember my passwords, but I know how to use the computer," he replied. "I just hope I have the passwords written down somewhere."

Dr. Weston nodded. "Again, you have your *procedural* memory—how to do things you're used to doing. You probably remember how to drive your car, how to mow the lawn, make your bed, and things of that nature—things that are second nature to you, that you can do without having to put a lot of thought into them. It's your *declarative* memory that's lost—personal episodes, relationships, who people are and who they are to you—that's missing." He shook his head. "I'm not a brain specialist—unfortunately there isn't one here at Woodbridge General. But there's a really good one in Fresno, and there's an excellent brain center at the UCLA Medical Center in Los Angeles. It would be a good idea for you to either see Dr. Gai in Fresno or have some tests done at UCLA. I've discussed this with your parents, of course—"

"University of California at Los Angeles," Eric said out loud.

Dr. Weston smiled. "Yes, that's UCLA. Very good."

Eric smiled back at the doctor. He felt better. As frustrating as it was, the memory loss was only temporary. It would come back, in time. He just had to be patient.

He closed his eyes, resting his head back on his pillow. Dr. Weston was still talking, but he wasn't listening anymore. *Why can I remember unimportant things like what UCLA stands for, but I can't recognize my own mother?*

"I was just telling Eric he'll be able to go home in a few days," Dr. Weston was saying.

Eric opened his eyes and saw Mom putting a green glass vase of red roses on a table on the other side of the room. She was smiling at him. "That's wonderful news, isn't it, Eric?"

She walked over to the side of his bed and picked up one of his hands.

I wish she wouldn't talk to me like I'm a baby, he thought.

"All your friends can't wait to see you," she went on, sitting down, not letting go of his hand. "Chris and Lacey both said they're going to stop by this afternoon, now that you can have visitors."

Chris and Lacey? Who the hell are Chris and Lacey?

As though reading his mind, she went on in a softer voice, "Chris has been your best friend ever since you were little boys—and Lacey's been your girlfriend for going on two years now." She leaned forward and stroked his forehead. "It's okay, baby, you'll remember them. You will."

She smelled vaguely of some flower, and stale coffee. He bit his lower lip to keep the frustration down. He knew she meant well, but it was annoying. He met Dr. Weston's eyes and the doctor winked at him. "I'll check in with you later, okay, Eric?"

Eric nodded and watched Dr. Weston walk out of his room. His mother picked up the remote and switched on the television, flipping through the channels. Eric closed his eyes. *I just want to be left alone*, he thought, trying to will her to go away. She started chattering—silence seemed to make her uncomfortable—about things she apparently thought he knew about or cared about. Stories about neighbors and other people in town he would have understood, maybe even laughed at, before the accident. He listened to her, droning on and on, his irritation growing.

She just doesn't get it or doesn't want to, he thought as she kept talking, oblivious to the fact he was neither reacting nor responding to anything she said.

And then he felt bad for feeling that way.

He opened his eyes and watched her. She wasn't looking at him or at the television set. She was paging through a glossy magazine in her lap, and there were bags under her eyes. There was something off about her hair, like she'd styled it in a hurry or just didn't care enough to do more than go through the motions. Her shoulders, exposed by the straps of the white tennis shirt she was wearing, seemed a little hunched, and he noticed her fingernails were painted but bitten down almost to the quick. She'd crossed her legs, and the elevated foot was swinging almost frantically back and forth. Her makeup wasn't right, either.

She looks like she colored outside the lines, he thought.

She stopped talking.

He smiled at her.

"Are you okay?" she asked in a low, quivery tone. Her tongue darted out and ran over her bottom lip. "Should I ring for the doctor, a nurse? Tell me what you need, Eric."

"I love you, Mom," he said, smiling. It wasn't true. He didn't remember her. He remembered nothing about her, nothing about their relationship. But he knew she needed to hear it, and he was glad he did once he saw the transformation.

Tears filled her eyes, and her mouth trembled. She reached out her hand. "Oh honey—"

Her hand touched his.

My poor baby, it breaks my heart to see you like this—but you're going to be fine, the doctor says so. You are going to remember everything, and all it takes is a trigger. I bet Chris and Lacey will do it. I would give anything to be going through this instead of you, and why couldn't it have been Danny? I know I'll go to hell for thinking that, but he's always been a problem, and you've always been such a good boy—

He pulled his hand away.

Her face had gone pale, her eyes widened.

They sat there, staring at each other, for what seemed an eternity.

"Danny?" He finally broke the silence. "Who's Danny?"

Her jaw dropped, and she slid her chair away from his bedside. Not far, just an inch or two, but enough for it to be noticeable.

She's afraid, he thought. *I've scared her. She was just thinking about Danny and I mentioned his name. She didn't say anything. She was THINKING it and somehow, somehow I knew.*

"Danny," she said, her voice quivering, "is your younger brother. He's at baseball practice right now, but he'll be coming by later on to see you." She cleared her throat. "He's been here almost every day, you know. He's sat here by your side." She forced a smile. "I—I think I'm going to go get another cup of coffee. Do you want a soda or anything, honey?" She stood up, backing away from his bed.

He smiled back at her. "I guess. I'm a little thirsty."

"I'll be right back." She kept backing away, like she was afraid to turn her back to him. Then she reached the door and was gone.

The television was on. A man with a microphone was talking to an audience of jeering people. An enormous woman was on the stage, missing a few teeth and with tattoos all over her fleshy arms. Her hair was dyed black, and when she talked he could barely understand her. A caption flashed beneath her face: TRACY THINKS HER HUSBAND IS SLEEPING WITH HER SISTER.

He closed his eyes again.

How could I have known what she was thinking?

It didn't make any sense.

The door opened and she walked back in, carrying a steaming cup of coffee in one hand and a red can in the other. She seemed to have recovered her composure somewhat, and she smiled as she passed the can to him. He looked at it, popped the top, and took a drink. She sat back down in her chair.

He swallowed and put the can down on the bedside table. "Will you tell me what happened?"

She didn't look at him. "What are you talking about?"

"The day of the accident," he replied, gesturing at his head. "Why did that policeman want to talk to me?"

"That's your Uncle Arnie." She took a drink of the coffee. "Your car went off the road. It's totaled, completely unsalvageable. It's okay, the insurance will help us buy you a new one—"

"Who's Sean Brody?"

She closed her eyes. "Eric—"

"Tell me," he commanded. "I have a right to know."

Her hand shook as she placed the coffee cup down on the table. "I wasn't home that day, Eric. I was playing tennis at the country club like I do every Tuesday afternoon. Your father was at work, and Danny was at baseball practice." She took a deep breath. "I got a call from the police when they found your car. Someone saw you go off the road and called for help. You were driving too fast—you lost control as you went around a curve in the road." She paused. "Sean—Sean was in the car with you. He was in the backseat. I don't know why you had him with you. You used to be friends with Sean, but when you boys got to high school something happened, I don't know, you never told your father and me anything about it, you just stopped being friends with him and he stopped coming over to the house."

"So, it wasn't normal he'd be in my car."

"That's one of the mysteries." She took another deep breath. "The other is, well, he'd been shot."

"Shot?" He stared at her, feeling his entire body going cold at the same time. "Someone shot him?"

"Apparently, he was in your backseat—the backseat was covered in his blood." She went on, "That's why the police wanted to talk to you, sweetie. No one knows anything. How he was shot, why, where—what was he doing in your car?" She shrugged and her face flooded with color. "Some people think you shot him—which of course is completely absurd."

"Is it?" he whispered, closing his eyes and trying to think, to remember.

"Of course it's absurd!" She became quite agitated. She got up and started pacing. "I'm not saying that because I'm your mother. Where would you have gotten a gun?" She walked back over to the bed, sitting down on the side—careful, he noticed, not to touch him—and folded her arms. "You were on your way into town, Eric, when you went off the road. No, the only thing that makes sense is you either saw it happen, or you found him, and were trying to get him to the hospital. That's why you were driving so fast—you've always been a very good driver—and why you lost control of the car. You were trying to get help for him."

He opened his eyes. *She's made up her mind*, he thought, *and nothing's going to change it. That's what she believes.*

If only I could believe it, too.

"I think I want to take a nap," he said, closing his eyes again, hoping she'd leave. "You don't have to stick around here."

"Maybe I'll go grab something to eat," she said nervously.

He nodded, and he didn't open his eyes again until he heard the door shut behind her.

Someone shot Sean Brody. He was in my car. He died. And I don't remember any of it.

He took a deep breath and closed his eyes. A nap wasn't such a bad idea—

"Eric? Are you awake?"

He sat up in the bed, rubbing his eyes and trying to get a look at the girl who was standing in the doorway.

She was so beautiful he thought at first he must be still

dreaming. But she stepped into the room and shut the door behind her, giving him a tentative smile. Her hair was honey-blond and thick, hanging down her back. She was petite, barely five feet tall, with a narrow waist and curvy hips accentuated by the low-cut jean shorts she was wearing. Her Woodbridge Wildcats T-shirt fit snugly across her chest. The sleeves were cut off, and the white cotton accentuated her golden tan. Her eyes were almond-shaped and framed with long lashes. As she hesitantly stepped closer to his bed he could see her eyes were brown flecked with gold. She wasn't wearing a lot of makeup, but her golden skin glowed with health. Her teeth were even and white. She stopped a few feet from his bed, chewing nervously on her lower lip. "I didn't mean to wake you up," she said in a low, throaty voice. "I can come back later if you'd rather go back to sleep."

"No, it's okay." He pushed himself up into a sitting position, catching his breath as the movement triggered some pain in his ribs. "You are…?"

Her eyes opened wide and her hand flew up to her mouth. "Oh my God, I didn't think—" She sank down into the chair hard, shaking her head. "I mean, I didn't think your mother was—oh, my God." The brown eyes shimmered with tears.

Here we go again, he thought, a little irritated. He took a deep breath, and pain stabbed through his ribs again. "I don't remember," he said flatly. "Anything."

She wiped at her eyes and forced a smile onto her face. "I'm sorry, Eric." She swallowed. "I'm Lacey. Lacey Tremayne. You don't—" She stopped herself. She exhaled and sat up more erect. "That must be so awful."

He shrugged. "It is what it is."

She gnawed on a fingernail. "Yeah." She was clearly nervous, like she would rather be somewhere, *anywhere*, else. "It must be frustrating."

"It is." He watched her as she continued worrying the fingernail. "I *want* to remember." He closed his eyes. "I don't recognize my own mother or father. I don't remember anything before waking up here in the hospital." He gestured around the room. "It's all a big blank—like there's this gray fog where my memories used to be. The weirdest thing"—he hesitated for just a moment—"is that I don't have *feelings*. I know I'm supposed to love my parents, right? That's normal. But I don't. I don't feel anything when I see my mom. I mean, I know she's my mother, but I don't feel anything when I look at her. She's a stranger to me."

"And you don't feel anything when you look at me?" Lacey half whispered.

He shook his head. "No." He smiled. "I just see a really pretty stranger."

"Your mother—" Lacey shook her head. "Your mother seemed to think I'd trigger some memories, or feelings, or something. That's why I agreed to come." She rubbed her eyes. "I thought—oh, never mind what I thought. It's really true, you don't remember." She stood up. "I'll let you get back to sleep."

"Don't go," Eric replied, watching her. She was really pretty. "The only people I've seen since I woke up are doctors and nurses and my mother. It's nice to have a pretty girl to talk to." *And maybe you'll answer some questions my mother wants to dodge.* "Please?"

She looked like she wanted to say no, but after a moment sat back down. "All right," she blew out a breath, forcing a smile onto her face that didn't quite reach her eyes, "what do you want to talk about?"

"Why did my mother think you'd trigger my memory?" He watched her face, the way her chest moved with her every breath.

She closed her eyes. "Because we'd been going steady since we were freshmen," she replied without opening her eyes. "And she doesn't know we broke up—or she knows and doesn't care."

"You were my girlfriend?" Eric grinned.

"Uh-huh." She nodded. "Until about a week before the accident. That's when we broke up."

"Why?"

"I don't know."

"You don't?"

"You broke up with me, Eric." She gripped the arms of the chair until her knuckles turned white. "You dumped me, and then you wouldn't talk to me anymore. You cut me off. You wouldn't give me a chance to explain—"

"Explain what?" He gave her a sheepish grin, raising his hands and shrugging. "Although you could tell me anything and I'd have to believe you."

In spite of herself, she laughed. "Well, that's certainly true, isn't it?" She pulled her chair closer to the bed. "I could brain you, you know." She shook her head again, the honey-blond hair bouncing and glinting as it caught the light. "You're finally talking to me again—but you'll probably stop when I tell you." She sighed, hugging herself. "I don't know if I should—I don't think it's a good idea to get you upset."

"Okay, why don't we just let it slide for now?" Eric replied. "I can't imagine any reason good enough to dump someone like you." He gave a half-shrug. "But then my imagination's not exactly working at top speed."

She laughed again, and he felt himself glowing inside. *That's something*, he thought. *I don't know what it is, but making her laugh makes me feel good. Maybe that's a start—maybe Mom was right. Being around her is good for me.*

"Well, I'd rather not talk about it. It's funny, I must have thought of a dozen things to say when I got the chance to talk to you again." She shook her head again. "This—I mean, it's so weird." She leaned forward. "I can't figure out any of it. It doesn't make any sense, Eric. Why was Sean in your car, anyway?" She held up her hand. "I know, you don't remember. I was just thinking out loud."

"Why is it so weird?" He watched her face. "Weren't we friends?"

"You used to be, back in junior high." She shrugged. "You and Chris and Sean were inseparable. You did everything together. But when we started high school—you and Chris weren't friends with Sean anymore. I don't know why—you would never really talk about Sean."

"What was Sean like?"

Her smile was sad. "I liked Sean. I thought he was a sweet guy. He was always so nice…" Her voice trailed off. "But something must have happened that summer before we started high school—after that he was kind of different. I mean, he was still sweet, but not as outgoing and friendly. He kept to himself most of the time—it's almost like he was a completely different person."

Eric scratched his forehead. "And I never talked about it?"

"No." She frowned, her forehead wrinkling as her eyebrows came together. "I mean, when I heard about the accident—and Sean—it didn't make any sense to me. It still doesn't." She shivered. "Why would anyone shoot Sean? He was"—she paused for a moment—"such a sweet guy. I knew you didn't do it, of course, even if—" She broke off and flushed a little, not meeting his eyes.

"Even if?" He prodded.

"You'll find out soon enough, I suppose." She sighed. "Some

people—idiots—think *you* shot him and your uncle is helping cover it up." Her eyes flashed with anger. "Which is just stupid. You could never do something like that. Never."

Hearing her say it was still a shock—even though it wasn't the first time he'd heard it. He swallowed and closed his eyes. *It's human nature, people talk. And it is weird. And you need to get used to hearing it—until they catch whoever shot him, there are going to be people who think you did it. Besides, it's not like you know for sure that you didn't shoot him.* He opened his eyes. "Thanks, Lacey, I appreciate it." He slammed his fist down into the mattress. "It's so frustrating! I can't even say for sure—"

"Stop it—don't even think it." Lacey reached over and grabbed his hand—

—I don't believe it for a minute. It's so nice to be sitting here, talking with you like old times. It broke my heart when you broke up with me. I still love you, and I could never believe you would shoot anyone. That's just crazy. I'm so sorry for what I did—maybe this is a chance for us to get back together and I can make things right. I'm so sorry—you have no idea! It will never happen again—

She pulled her hand back as though burned. Her face turned pale beneath the tan and her eyes widened. "What—*what the hell was that?*"

Eric looked at her for a moment before he answered. "You cheated on me with my best friend?"

"You remember?" Her voice was tiny. "Eric, I'm so sorry." She started crying. "You never gave me a chance to explain—"

He closed his eyes and let his head drop back down onto the pillow. He knew he should be hurt and angry, but he didn't feel anything. "So explain." He opened his eyes and looked at her.

She wiped at her face. "Eric…" She took a moment to compose herself. "It was a big mistake—I've regretted it ever since. I don't know what I was thinking. I wasn't thinking. I've tried to figure it out ever since and I just can't…I can't figure it out." She held up her hands helplessly. "You weren't here. Your family had driven down to Santa Barbara for the weekend, and I went to a party with Connie and—" She broke off. "Connie Hansen and Brenda Davis—they're my best friends. There was a party out at the Ledge, and I didn't want to go, but they talked me into going. I should have just stayed home."

He tried to picture Connie and Brenda in his head, but he couldn't. There was nothing there, just a blank wall like every time he tried to remember anything. It was frustrating.

"There was beer." She shook her head. "I don't usually drink—I'm not blaming the beer, but I drank too much and was feeling lonely, so I wandered off into the woods to be by myself, and Chris followed me to make sure I was all right." She shrugged. "I started crying because I missed you, and the next thing I knew we were kissing." She started crying again. "That's all there was to it, Eric, I swear. But I couldn't not tell you—we never lied to each other—and you just looked at me and asked me for your class ring back." She took a deep breath. "And that was the last time you ever talked to me. You wouldn't take my calls, you wouldn't answer my messages, nothing. I swear, Eric, it wasn't anything and if I could take it back—"

"Stop, please." He waved his hand tiredly. "I don't—I don't want to hear any more."

"Eric, please—"

I should feel something, he thought, *but I don't. That's not right. It's not normal.* "Lacey," he said out loud, "it's okay. Really, don't worry about it."

"But you remembered," she said in a small voice. "That's good, isn't it? I mean, you remembered something?"

He turned his head to look at her. "I don't remember. Anything."

"But—"

"When you touched me—" He stopped. It sounded crazy. "I could read your mind."

"That—that's not possible," Lacey replied. "It's not. You remembered."

"I don't remember anything!" he half shouted, feeling his temper rising. "Can't you get that through your head? I don't remember anything! I can't remember! You're a total stranger to me, don't you get it? Doesn't anybody get it?" His temper took complete control. "You have no idea what it's like! Everyone comes in here and I don't know who anyone is! I don't even recognize my own goddamned mother!" He pressed his fists to his forehead. "They can't even tell me if I am *ever going to remember anything*!"

As quickly as it had come, the anger drained out of him.

"I'm sorry," she whispered. She stood up, wiping at her eyes. "About everything."

"Lacey—"

The door shut behind her.

He stared at the ceiling. *That went well*, he thought bitterly.

He thought back, replaying the conversation in his mind.

People think I killed Sean.

Maybe, he reflected, *maybe I did.*

He blinked away tears.

I might be a murderer.

CHAPTER THREE

The car pulled up into a driveway. "Here we are," his mother said, smiling brightly at him. "Aren't you glad to be home?"

The last few days had passed in a blur. They reduced the amount of painkiller he was taking—but continued to poke and prod and do tests. Since he was awake most of the time, he found himself watching a lot of television and reading magazines his mother brought for him. She also kept up an almost nonstop string of chatter—he knew she was just trying to trigger his memory, but it was frustrating listening to her talk about people and events he couldn't remember. Several times he felt his temper slipping out of control, but just closed his eyes and tried to tune her out. It wasn't fair to her, he knew, for him to get angry and yell at her to shut up, no matter how badly he wanted to. And if he somehow managed to stay in control—eventually she would have to go get a drink or use the bathroom, or a nurse would show up to take him on a walk around the halls. He wasn't in much pain from his ankle anymore, but they still made him use crutches. His father stopped by to see him every day after work. The first time he showed up, Eric was alone and had no idea who the stranger coming into his room was. He felt bad when he saw the hurt in his father's eyes.

He had other visitors too—an endless stream of friends from school he didn't recognize, and he hated seeing the pity in their eyes when they talked to him about things he couldn't remember—parties and proms and dances, football games and classes. He knew they meant well, but it was aggravating—he soon learned all he had to do to get rid of them was close his eyes and say he was tired. It worked every time—and he tried not to notice their obvious relief to get away.

The visits were awkward and uncomfortable. No one mentioned the accident or the dead body found in his car. No one said the name of the dead boy. He thought it strange until he figured out his mother was warning them before letting them into his room. She'd leave the room to give them privacy—but she always left the door open and he could see her sitting in a chair in the hall, listening and ready to swoop in if the conversation took a turn she didn't like.

So he didn't bother bringing any of it up himself, even though he wanted to.

It was bad enough he didn't know who any of his visitors were.

He didn't want to believe he was a killer.

So the visits turned into something to be endured, like X-rays and blood draws. There was a pattern to them. They all would come in and introduce themselves. He'd smile and thank them for coming. Their names meant nothing to him—Connie Hansen, Jemal Washington, Lisa Carter, Bobby Wheeler, Jon or Tom or Becky whatever. Girls he didn't recognize would lean down and kiss his cheek, saying things like "you'll get better soon" or some well-meaning but lame-sounding variation of the same thing. The boys would lightly punch his shoulder or just stand back and look a little stricken, asking if he was going to be able to play football.

Apparently he was important to the team—he played fullback, and was the team's leading rusher.

One kid, Jeremy Glass, looked stricken when he said he wasn't sure if he'd be able to play. "We need you, man," he pleaded. "No way we can win the conference without you in the backfield."

Jeremy kept shifting his weight from one foot to the other. He wouldn't look Eric in the eyes either. Eric found himself growing irritated, wanting to scream at him, *If you didn't want to come, why did you?*

And then it hit him in a flash: *He thinks I killed that kid.*

Which made all of the other awkward visits make sense.

His classmates, friends, people he'd known all of his life, weren't sure if he was, in fact, a killer.

Jeremy was still talking, but he wasn't listening anymore.

My friends, the people who know me best, aren't sure. What does that say about me as a person? Who was I? What kind of person was—AM—I?

Eric closed his eyes and claimed he was tired, waiting until he heard the door shut behind Jeremy before opening them again.

His mother walked back in with a cup of coffee in one hand and a tired smile on her face. She sat down in the chair next to his bed like she always did, and before she could say anything he just turned his head away, closed his eyes, and feigned sleep. He heard her stand up and then felt her hand brushing his hair off his forehead. He felt her lips press against his forehead.

Lacey never came back.

He wondered why Chris Moore—his best friend—never showed up.

He slept with your girlfriend, that's why. Some best friend.

He also noticed the nurses were acting differently around him—ever since the whole thing about Nurse Latrice's apartment catching fire. They were still polite but seemed more distant, almost afraid to touch him.

He'd certainly scared Lacey. How had he known about her and Chris?

That hadn't been a memory.

He knew it when their hands touched. It was like he could see into her mind—but only when their hands were touching. She'd felt something too—she'd pulled back away from him.

But that wasn't possible.

But he'd known about the fire in Latrice's apartment. That wasn't possible, either. That was why the nurses seemed a little afraid of him.

He didn't know what to think.

Dr. Weston, though, didn't act differently. He wanted to ask him about it, but not in front of his mother. And she was always there, sitting in her chair, watching and listening, asking questions. He was starting to feel trapped. So, when Dr. Weston had announced he could go home the next day, he was relieved. He didn't remember home, but it had to be better than this antiseptic-smelling reality, which was all he did know. And maybe his mother wouldn't feel the need to sit in a chair next to his bed all day, every day.

At least he hoped that would be the case.

And now he was home.

"I'm glad to be out of the hospital." He opened the car door with a grimace and stood up, leaning on the car. The ankle no longer hurt—it was taped up with an elastic bandage and he could put all of his weight on it. Every once in a while it would twinge—nothing painful, it was more like the ankle making sure he still knew it wasn't completely healed.

He'd hoped as the car wound through the small town his memory would be triggered. It hadn't happened, not once.

Nothing seemed familiar—none of the stores or gas stations or fast food places with their enormous signs, none of the names on the street signs. His hopes had dwindled completely when she turned into a driveway and turned off the car. The house wasn't familiar—he recognized nothing.

He stood there, looking at pine trees and the lush overgrown lawn, the birdbath in the center of the front yard, the metal mailbox on a long wooden post at the foot of the drive, and it was like he'd never been there before. He looked at the house—a two-story gabled house painted yellow with brown trim, with brown shutters open at every window and a porch that ran the length of the front—and he felt absolutely nothing inside. The garage doors were shut, and he closed his eyes, searching through his mind—nothing but a gray fog that obscured everything.

He shut the car door. There was a cast on his wrist—the strangers who'd visited his room at the hospital had signed it with a black Sharpie his mother kept in her purse—writing little messages, some of which made no sense to him. Dr. Weston had also taped his ribs to help them heal, but the tape didn't stop them from aching from time to time. His pain pills were in his mother's purse. He'd taken one before they left the hospital—he hated being wheeled out to the curb in a wheelchair by a nurse, but they'd given him no choice—and his mind was a little foggy from it. But the house—his *home*—he'd swear he'd never seen it before.

He could feel the frustration coming again, and he closed his eyes for a moment and pushed it away. "It's perfectly normal for someone in your position," Dr. Weston had insisted, time after time. "Don't feel bad about it. It's normal, it's healthy."

But hearing that didn't make it any easier.

Sometimes he just wanted to scream, to pound his fists on something, anything. He knew it wouldn't make him feel any better, wouldn't fix his memory or bring it back, help him to remember his life—or what happened the day of the accident.

He couldn't forget a body had been in his car.

He didn't know why his uncle hadn't come back to question him some more—*maybe because he knows it's hopeless*—and he hated the way his mother would change the subject whenever he tried to bring it up.

Am I the kind of person who would kill someone? He couldn't stop wondering, wanting to ask, but he could never bring himself to say the words.

Because you're afraid of how they might answer.

He swallowed, fighting down the frustrated feeling yet again.

His mother hadn't stopped talking when he got out of the car. He nodded but wasn't listening, had no idea what she was talking about. "I'm so glad you're finally home," she said, a bright smile on her face as she shut her car door, her eyes glistening with tears.

Feeling guilty for not listening, he turned away, unable to look her in the eyes. He took a deep breath. The air smelled of fresh pine. He could see a forest of pine trees beyond the house, climbing up an incline. There were clouds gathered around the top of the mountain, and for a brief moment he saw a rainbow before it faded away completely. A loud noise from down the street startled him. *Someone's started a lawn mower*, he thought with a grin. He knew the sound—that was a memory not lost in the gray mist inside his head. He closed his eyes. The car chirped—*she turned on the car alarm*—and he smiled.

It was *something*.

He took another deep breath as he followed her up the walk to the front porch, looking at the wide lawn, the rosebushes, trying to see something, anything, that would trigger a chord in his mind. But none of it looked familiar. He limped up the steps to the wide porch at the front of the house. There were wooden rocking chairs, a table, and a porch swing. She unlocked the front door and held it open for him.

The television was on, and a boy of about thirteen was draped over the couch, reading a magazine. He didn't look up until Mom said, "Danny!"

Danny scowled and sat up. "Welcome home," he said in a monotone, clearly not meaning it.

"Thanks." Eric smiled back at him, but Danny's scowl didn't soften. Eric limped over to a reclining chair and sat down. Danny watched him. Danny had brown hair, worn long and lifeless. His face was dotted with angry red pimples, his eyes practically hidden by a huge pair of glasses. There were braces on his teeth, and his body looked soft. He was wearing a baggy T-shirt and a pair of shorts.

"Danny, you have baseball practice in a few hours, and I asked you to mow the lawn." Mom walked briskly through the living room. "What are you waiting for? Get a move on!"

"Why do I have to mow the lawn?" he whined. "It's not my chore. It's not fair!"

She stopped at the doorway to the kitchen, and put both hands on her hips. "Get used to it! Life's not fair! I told you to mow the lawn, now do it!"

Danny's scowl deepened. "Do I have to?"

"I can help," Eric said.

"Don't be silly, Eric," she went on. "You need to get some rest. Go on up to your room, and Danny, I better not have to tell you again, do you understand me?" She disappeared through the door.

Danny made another face at Eric and stomped out the front door. Eric sighed and leaned back in his chair.

My brother doesn't seem to like me very much, he mused. *I wonder why?* He got up and walked over to a wall where photographs had been hung. There were a lot of pictures of him—more so than of his brother. Professional photographs, some of the family together, some of him in his football uniform. There were photographs of him and Lacey, laughing and happy. There was one of the two of them—he was wearing a tux, she was wearing a sea-green dress with a corsage—that held his interest. He closed his eyes and tried to remember it being taken.

Nothing.

He turned his back and headed to the stairs. He climbed up to the second floor, not recognizing the hallway. He walked down the hallway, looking in doors. A bathroom, several bedrooms, and a linen closet.

He paused in the doorway to the room at the end of the hall.

There was something—almost familiar about the room. He closed his eyes, tried to grasp the fragment of feeling in his mind, but it slipped away.

This must be my room, he thought as he stood in the doorway. He flipped the light switch and hesitantly walked in. The walls were covered with framed photographs—some of them duplicates of the ones on the living room walls. There were also some frames with spaces for multiple snapshots, and those he looked at closely. He recognized himself in groups of kids, or alone with Lacey, with Lacey and Chris, sometimes just with Chris. Some of the pictures were from what he took to be school, others in the woods, some where everyone mugged for the camera on the shore of a stream or river.

He didn't recognize any of the places, and the only face he recognized was Lacey's.

He walked over to the bookcase and ran his fingers along the book spines. He read some of the titles: *The Adventures of Tom Sawyer*, *The Adventures of Huckleberry Finn*, *As I Lay Dying*, among others. None of them looked like they had been read; they looked brand new. The bottom shelf held stacks of comic books—Spider-Man, Batman, Superman, Justice League of America, Teen Titans, and Green Lantern.

He didn't remember any of them.

He bit his lip and sighed, feeling his spirits sink. He'd been so hoping that coming home would do the trick—but he was no better off now than he was in the hospital.

"At least it doesn't smell like antiseptic in here," he said out loud, and grinned. He walked over to his desk. It was pushed up against a wall, and directly over it was hung a poster of a beautiful woman in a skimpy bathing suit. He stared at her but had no idea who she was. She was smiling at the camera, her lips slightly pouting.

He shook his head and pulled open the desk drawer. It was crammed full of a mishmash of miscellany—pens, pencils, a pencil sharpener, loose paper, scissors, a stapler, paper clips. He closed it.

The surface of the desk was clear except for a large thin book bound in purple leather. His name was stamped in gold in the lower left corner: *Eric Matthews*. The words *Woodbridge High* were written across the top in black. In the center was a gold outline of a big cat roaring.

His yearbook.

He picked it up and sat down on the bed, opening it.

The inside cover was full of handwritten messages.

Eric—was a blast having Chemistry with you, hope we have some classes together next year, love Ellen

Go Wildcats! Let's take State next year! Your friend Jeremy

One more year and we're off to college! Thanks for being such a great friend, Josh Harrison

Eric—to the best fullback in the history of Woodbridge High! It's been great cheering for you and being your friend, always, Connie Hansen

Eric: I can't believe it's summer already. I hope we get to have our lockers next to each other again next year! And if you ever get tired of Lacey, give me a call! Hugs and kisses, Tessa Doyle

Eric—too cool for school! Bobby Morris

He started leafing through the glossy pages of photographs.

Every page had words scrawled in ink and signed with names he didn't know. He flipped through the senior class photographs until he reached a page that said JUNIOR CLASS.

There was single photograph on that page, labeled JUNIOR CLASS OFFICERS.

He looked at his own smiling face. He was wearing a football jersey with the number 12 on it. He had one arm around Lacey and his other arm around a taller boy, who was also wearing a football jersey with 8 on it. Lacey was wearing a sweater with a big *W* on it over a short pleated skirt. There were two girls, dressed exactly like Lacey, kneeling in front of the three of them. They'd both visited him in the hospital.

He read the caption.

BOTTOM ROW: Treasurer Connie Hansen, Student Council Rep Bev Rossiter

STANDING: Secretary Lacey Tremayne, President Eric Matthews, Vice President Chris Moore

I was class president? He scratched his head.

He examined Chris Moore's face. This was his best friend— the friend who'd slept with his girlfriend when he'd been out of town.

Chris was good looking. He was about three or four inches taller than Eric, with broad shoulders and muscular arms. His hair was blond, his whole face lit up with a smile. He was resting his hands on Bev Rossiter's shoulders, and her head was tilted up and a little sideways, smiling up at Chris.

Chris, though, was looking straight at the camera.

We look really close, Eric thought, *the three of us.*

He turned the page, running his finger down the list of names till he found the one he wanted.

Sean Brody.

He stared at Sean's face. He had shoulder-length blond hair, parted in the middle. He wasn't smiling at the camera—his lips were a grim set line across his thin face. The hair was thick, the lips narrow, the nose straight. His eyes were his most arresting feature—big and expressive. His head was slightly tilted to one side, and his facial expression made it clear he would have rather been anywhere else than posing for that picture.

What happened? Eric wondered as he traced the outline of the picture with his finger. *Why were you in my car? Did I shoot you? If I did, why would I do such a thing?*

He started flipping through the pages quickly, reading everything, trying to find what Sean had written, thinking there might be a clue in it.

But he didn't see Sean's signature anywhere. He turned to

the back and looked at the end pages. He hadn't signed there, either. He started working forward from the back. The last ten pages were taken up with ads, and while kids had written all over them, there was nothing from Sean there, either.

Lacey had taken a full page for herself, writing about dates and dances and parties and what must have been private jokes between the two of them. She'd drawn hearts all over the page, even dotting her i's with hearts. It was clear from her words that she loved him. She talked about their future plans, about how great their senior year was going to be, and maybe going to college together when the time came.

She signed it *I will always love you, Lacey.*

So, what had happened? Why had she slept with Chris? His best friend?

He shook his head and kept working his way through the yearbook, past activities and clubs, until he got to the athletic teams.

He paused when he got to the Homecoming pictures.

There he stood, on the football field with his helmet under his arm, his other arm linked with Lacey Tremayne, who was wearing a long dress and had a tiara on her head. In her free arm she held a long-stemmed red rose.

JUNIOR PRINCE ERIC MATTHEWS AND PRINCESS LACEY TREMAYNE.

He looked serious, in contrast to Lacey's big smile. There were two thick black lines drawn under his eyes.

Another picture, a boy and a girl with crowns on their heads sitting on thrones, and he and Lacey were standing to their right, with their crowns. He wasn't in his football uniform anymore—in this one he was wearing a suit and tie. On the other side of the thrones another boy and girl stood, with crowns on their heads.

HOMECOMING COURT: Sophomore Attendants Ryan Fielding and Debby Murray, King Timothy Lambert and Queen Becky Cochrane, Junior Prince Eric Matthews and Junior Princess Lacey Tremayne.

In this picture, he was beaming at the camera.

"Revisiting past triumphs?" Danny sneered from the doorway.

Eric closed the book and smiled at his brother. "I'm just trying to remember." He sighed. "It sucks to not remember anything."

"Whatever."

"Huh?" Eric stared at him. "Why did you say that?"

"It means you aren't fooling *me*, Eric," Danny said with scorn, crossing his arms and leaning against the door frame. "You can fool Mom and your doctor and Dad and everybody else, but you don't fool me. You never have. They all think you're the golden child, so perfect and wonderful. But I know you—much better than they do."

"Danny, I don't know—"

"Just knock it off already." Danny interrupted him. "Don't pull that crap with *me*, Eric, okay? God, you piss me off. You're going to get away with it, too—just like you *always* get away with everything."

"What—"

"Give it up already." Danny crossed his arms. "You killed Sean, Eric. Admit it! You're just faking amnesia so you can get away with it. You should be in jail. But everyone feels sorry for you instead."

"I'm not—"

"You're a killer," Danny snapped. "You hated Sean Brody— that's something Mom and Dad and Uncle Arnie don't know. But I do. I saw how you treated him."

Eric froze. "How did I treat him?"

Danny rolled his eyes. "For God's sake, Eric—you treated him like garbage. You used to make fun of him all the time. I guess he must have finally done something to really set you off, and you killed him. And perfect Eric, the perfect student and football star, is going to get away with it, like he always does."

He slammed the bedroom door.

Chapter Four

E ric sat there for a moment, staring at the door.
My brother thinks I'm a killer.
He felt like he'd been slapped in the face.

He lay back on the bed, still holding the yearbook in his trembling hands.

But it's what you've wanted to know, isn't it? Are you capable of killing someone? If your brother thinks so, it must be true. Who would know you better than your brother?

A lawn mower roared to life in front of the house.

"He hates me," he said out loud, still holding on to the yearbook. "My own brother hates me."

It wasn't supposed to be that way, he knew that much. Brothers might argue, fight, get on each other's nerves, but underneath it all they were supposed to love each other. He got off the bed and put the yearbook back on the desk. He looked over the books on the bookcase. The second shelf held a complete set of *World Book Encyclopedias*, the third what appeared to be a complete set of Hardy Boys mysteries; a bunch of other titles, paperbacks he didn't remember reading by authors whose names meant nothing to him, filled the next shelf. In the corner of the room was a stack of magazines, with the *Sports Illustrated* swimsuit issue on the very top. Atop the bookcase sat two other yearbooks, but he didn't see any point in looking at those.

He walked over to the closet and pulled the door open. He stepped inside and started looking through the clothes. Sweaters, jeans, pullover and button-down shirts. A couple of football jerseys, shoes neatly paired up on the floor, jackets and coats hung in the corner. He pulled out a purple jacket with gold leather sleeves. A big gold *W* had been sewn onto the right breast. On the left part of the *W* was a gold football with three gold bars beneath it. On the right was a pair of gold crossed baseball bats, with three bars underneath them. Out of curiosity he checked one pocket, and when it turned out to be empty he stuck his hand in the other, finding an open pack of Dentyne. He hung the jacket back up. He turned off the overhead light and stepped back into the bedroom.

He took a deep breath and scanned the room again.

It might as well have been the hospital room.

He walked over to the window and opened the blinds. Danny was angrily pushing the lawn mower over the grass, his face red and sweaty. His lips were moving, like he was mumbling to himself. As Eric watched, he didn't make the turn around the birdbath wide enough and mowed down some flowers. He didn't even pause, he just kept moving. The back of his white T-shirt was drenched in sweat, and his sweaty legs were covered with grass mulch.

Why do you hate me, Danny? he wondered as Danny mowed the grass around the massive pine tree near the road. There was a loud grinding sound as he ran over a big pine cone, and shards flew out from the side of the mower. Again, Danny didn't stop, just struggled to maneuver the mower. A woman jogged by on the road, her hair pulled back into a ponytail, wearing just a pair of shorts and a sports bra, her eyes hidden by dark sunglasses.

Something glimmered in the back of his mind, but when he tried to grab on to it, it faded away to nothing.

As he watched, a huge blue pickup truck turned into the driveway. It was filthy; dried mud was spattered all over the doors and the sides of the truck. He couldn't see the driver because the windows were tinted. The driver's side door opened, and a teenager got out.

Chris, he thought, recognizing him from the yearbook pictures. Danny waved at him, and Chris waved back. He was wearing a red football jersey with the sleeves cut off and paint spatters all over the front. His bare, tanned arms and shoulders were thickly muscled. His hair was cut short and spiky, and like the jogger's, his eyes were hidden behind sunglasses. Without looking up at the window, Chris walked up the path to the porch.

Eric lay back down on the bed and heard the doorbell ringing over the blast of the lawnmower. He closed his eyes and waited.

A few moments later, there was a soft knock on his door. "Eric?" a male voice asked, barely above a whisper.

"Come in." He opened his eyes and scooted up so he was sitting, his back against his pillows and the headboard.

"Hey there, bud." Chris grinned as he entered the room. He'd taken off his sunglasses and hooked them in the front of his shirt. "Finally home, huh?" He pulled out the desk chair, turned it around, and sat down, propping his feet up on the bed. "How you feeling? You must be glad to be out of the hospital."

"Yeah." Eric shrugged, watching Chris's face. "I'm doing okay. Adjusting."

"Still not remembering anything?" Chris's grin got wider, and Eric noticed he had braces on his teeth. "Man, that's gotta suck—although there's a lot of things I wish I didn't remember."

"Yeah, it does suck," Eric agreed. He ran his hand over his buzzed hair. "It's driving me nuts."

"Man, they sure did a number on your hair." Chris laughed. "It'll grow back, right?"

"I had a concussion," Eric replied. "They had to shave it to make sure—you know."

"Sorry I didn't make it to the hospital after you, you know, you came to." Chris blew out a breath. "I went by a lot when you were unconscious. But I started working—my jerk parents made me get a job, can you believe that shit? My dad says he's tired of me freeloading and it's time to get a job." His eyes flashed angrily for a moment. "But it's not too bad—I'm lifeguarding at the country club. I get paid to sit up in the chair and watch babes in bathing suits splash around and get wet." He winked. "They like to flirt with me, too—guess they can't resist my manly bare chest." He grinned again. "Anyway, my shift is from eleven to seven, so I always was missing visiting hours. I wanted to be there, though, man."

"It's okay," Eric said. "I don't remember anything from before the accident."

"That's just crazy, man." Chris's eyes widened. "Nothing? I mean, I heard that, but it's crazy. You don't remember anything? You don't remember me?"

"No," Eric closed his eyes. "If I hadn't looked in the yearbook when I got home I'd have no idea who you are."

"Man, that's nuts!" Chris made a face. "That's got to totally suck, man."

"Try living it sometime," Eric snapped, sharper than he'd intended.

Chris flinched and he flushed under his tan. "Sorry," he mumbled.

"It's okay, sorry." Eric waved his hand. "It's just rough sometimes. I shouldn't be taking it out on you. It's not your fault. I'm glad to see you—even if I don't remember you." He laughed.

Chris laughed, too. "I can't even imagine how rough it must be—not even your parents?"

Eric shook his head. "They're strangers. Everyone is a stranger."

"Lacey said she came to see you." Chris started fidgeting with his class ring, not looking at Eric. "Look, man, I'm sorry about that, really, I don't know what I was thinking. You don't pull that kind of shit on a friend."

"It's okay." Eric felt tired. "I don't remember. Maybe when my memory comes back"—*Don't you mean if?*—"maybe I'll get mad about it. But," he frowned, "I mean, we must have talked about it before the accident. Lacey said I broke up with her but I didn't say why, so I must have known, right?"

Chris nodded. "Yeah." He took a deep breath and looked up. "We talked about it when you and your folks got back from your trip. I couldn't keep that from you, man." He sighed. "We were both drunk. I know that's not an excuse, there's no excuse—I'm a lowlife, I know, I've been trying to figure out ever since what the hell my problem is, why I would do something like that to my best friend, I mean, you're like a brother to me, you always have been, we've been buddies since we were kids—"

"Did I get mad?" It was weird, he thought, talking about something like this that *should* be upsetting, *should* make him mad, fighting mad, as dispassionately as if it happened to someone else. *But it kind of did happen to someone else, it happened to me* before, *and that might as well be a different person.*

"Mad? I don't know if *mad* is the right word." Chris

swallowed. "You didn't talk to me the whole week before— before the accident." He smiled faintly. "This is the first time you've talked to me since I told you."

Eric nodded. "So, we weren't friends anymore."

"You were *mad* at me. We were—*are*—still friends. I mean, at least I hoped we were. We go back too far, man, to let some stupid mistake turn us into enemies. You're my best friend, man. I think of you like a brother." He shook his head. "That whole week sucked for me—and then when I heard about the wreck…" His voice trailed off for a moment, and when he spoke again his voice was low and soft. "People kept saying you were going to die at first, and I couldn't believe I wouldn't get a chance to make it up to you, you know? And then you were in a coma." He swallowed. "It was *awful.*"

"You said I didn't talk to you the week before the accident? So, this thing"—he couldn't think of a better way to put it—"with you and Lacey happened about a week before I crashed?"

"Yeah." Chris leaned back in his chair, closing his eyes and tilting his head back. "It was the weekend before the wreck. You and your folks went away for the weekend and came home on Monday. I talked to you about it that night after the baseball game. You crashed on a Friday." Chris looked away from him. "I was scared you weren't going to wake up, my friend—everyone was. You scared the crap out of all of us." He stopped for a moment before adding in a lower voice, "I couldn't stand the thought of you—you know—without us ever getting the chance to make things right, you know?"

"So you don't know what was going on with me for the week or so before the accident?" Eric watched his face.

Chris shook his head. "No, man, I don't. You wouldn't answer my texts or e-mails, you wouldn't take my calls."

So he doesn't know anything. Neither would Lacey. What was I doing?

"Do you think—" Eric swallowed, and then forced the words out in a rush, "do you think I killed Sean Brody?"

"Dude!" Chris's eyes opened wide. "Don't even say that, as a joke, man! There's no way! No way you could ever do something like that!"

Eric forced a smile on his face. "Thanks," he said quietly. "That's good to hear."

"Don't even think it for a minute, man." Chris sat up straighter and leaned forward. "You'd never do something like that, you know? All the years we've been friends, you've never even gotten into a *fight.* You'd never do something like that—and why would you kill Sean anyway? I can't figure out what he was doing in your car in the first place, man. We didn't hang out with him anymore."

"Why didn't we?" Eric asked. "My mom said we all used to be tight. What happened?"

"Sean was a fag, man." Chris's face twisted. "That's why."

A fag. "You mean he was gay?" Eric said slowly.

And why would that matter?

A memory—*something*—was trying to push through the fog.

He was standing outside. There were trees everywhere. It was hot—the sun was beating down and he was sweating. The air was still. There was someone standing in front of him—Sean—it was Sean, and he was pale. "Eric, we used to be friends," he said, glancing nervously around. "But I know you're right. It's gone too far. I'm getting scared. But I don't know what to do."

And then it was gone.

He balled his fists and slammed them down on the bed. "Damn it!" he swore.

"It's okay, Eric." Chris reached out and grabbed his hand—

And there was a click, like there had been when Lacey touched his hand.

I'm so sorry about Lacey. I'm so glad you woke up, you didn't die, so I can make it up to you, but I'm also kind of glad you don't remember—

Chris pulled his hand back. "What the hell?" he whispered, his eyes wide, his face pale beneath the tan. "What just happened?"

Eric opened his mouth, but remembered the nurses and how they'd acted around him after the Latrice thing, and stopped himself from saying anything. "What are you talking about?" he asked, trying to keep his voice from shaking. *Stay calm, whatever you do, stay calm and pretend it didn't happen.* "I just felt a shock. No big deal."

"It was—" Chris shuddered, and shook his head. "Yeah, you're right, it was nothing. It was just—just a surprise." He smiled weakly.

"Why did we stop being friends with Sean?"

"I told you, he was a fag." Chris rubbed his hand with the other. "I told you."

The way he said it, Eric could tell he was supposed to be revolted. But he wasn't. "You have to tell me all of it." Eric closed his eyes again. "Please, Chris." He started to reach for his friend's hand, but stopped himself. "No one will tell me anything. It's driving me crazy thinking I might have killed him."

And what the hell is the deal with me touching people's hands and being able to read their minds? What is that all about? Could I do it before the accident, or is it something that's changed because of the accident?

He didn't like it. It made him feel like a freak.

"I told you, man, you couldn't have," Chris replied. "There's no way, Eric, it's just not possible. You wouldn't do something like that."

"*Somebody* shot him. And how did he wind up in my car?" Eric closed his eyes. "None of it makes any sense. Lacey said Sean and I weren't friends—you say the same thing. So why was he with me? How did he get in my car?"

"There's got to be an explanation." Chris shook his head. "I don't know what it is, but there has to be."

"Help me, Chris." Eric opened his eyes. "You're my best friend. Help me." He took a deep breath. "What—what are people saying?"

"Eric—" Chris looked away.

"Tell me," he insisted. "I have to know. I have a right to know." He laughed bitterly. "I'll find out eventually, and I'd rather be prepared. People are saying I did it, aren't they?"

"Well, nobody has said anything directly to me—you know, everyone knows we're brothers, man," Chris replied slowly. "But I hear things, you know? Like I said, I'm working for the rest of the summer as a lifeguard at the country club pool—people forget you're up there on the guard station—and I hear things." He sighed. "A lot of people think you killed him— but *only* because it's the easy explanation. That's what people are saying." He punched his leg. "But your friends—your friends don't think so. Nobody who really knows you thinks it."

"I don't even know who I was," Eric replied, feeling tears of frustration rising in his eyes. He wiped them away angrily.

"You were—you *are*—a great guy is what," Chris insisted. "Eric, you rarely ever got mad at anyone, no matter what. You never said anything bad about anyone. Never, not even when we were kids."

"What about Sean?" Eric closed his eyes again, hearing Chris's words again: *He was a fag.*

"That was more me than you," Chris admitted. "You wanted to still be friends with him. I was the one who—who talked you out of it."

"But why, Chris? What did it matter if he was"—he couldn't bring himself to say *fag*; somehow he knew it wasn't a nice word—"gay?"

"It's better that you don't remember. I wish I didn't."

"Tell me," Eric insisted. "You have to, Chris. If Sean and I haven't been friends since we got to high school, how did he end up in my car? It has to matter, Chris. I have to know. And you're the only person who can tell me."

"Man, I really don't—" Chris pleaded.

"You want me to forget about you and Lacey?"

Chris just stared at him, his mouth open.

"Then do this. Tell me why we stopped being friends with Sean, and I'll never ever mention the Lacey thing to you ever again. It'll be like it never happened." Eric folded his arms and waited.

Chris took a deep breath. "All right, then." And he started talking.

The three of them had been friends since kindergarten, did everything together. Pee Wee football, Little League, swim lessons—if one of them did it, they all did it. They were in Boy Scouts together. They camped out, spent the night at each other's houses—and then everything changed.

"In eighth grade, really, we started getting interested in girls—well, you and I did, Sean didn't." Chris went on. "Sean used to get mad at us for hanging out with girls. I—we didn't think anything about it—we just figured he would eventually get interested like we were, get a girlfriend, and then all of us would keep hanging out together. You know, with our girlfriends. But Sean was *jealous* of our girlfriends. He was mean to them—I think you were going steady with Connie Hansen then, I was going with Rita Lester—and he would pick on them, make fun of them. He made Connie cry once—that's one of the few times I ever saw you get mad. You two didn't talk to each other for a long time—that's why we decided to have the campout after school let out—try to get you and Sean to patch things up. But it didn't work out the way any of us had hoped it would, you know?" Chris shot a glance at him. "You don't remember any of this? None of it sounds familiar to you?"

Eric shook his head. "No."

"When we were camping out, you know, roasting hot dogs and marshmallows over the fire, it was just like old times." Chris went on, "We were just laughing and joking like nothing ever happened, you know? Sean even apologized for making Connie cry, it was all good. And then we got into our sleeping bags and went to sleep." His voice shook. "And in the middle of the night Sean got into my sleeping bag with me and he—" He stopped talking. "I screamed bloody murder, woke you up, starting hitting him, punching him...you pulled me off him, he was crying and saying he was sorry, he didn't know what was wrong with him and—" Chris covered his face in his hands. "He got his stuff and went home. You were the one who stuck up for him. You were the one who said it was okay, I overreacted—but I said we couldn't be friends with him anymore—and if you were his friend you couldn't be mine. So we—" He choked for a moment, and then got a hold of himself. "So we stopped being friends, but we promised each other we would never tell anyone. And that was it. We weren't friends anymore."

"We turned our backs on him?" Eric stared at him. He didn't like the sound of that. It—it was *wrong*.

"I know." Chris wiped at his eyes. "Ever since they found Sean—I don't know, Eric, all I can do is remember what he used to be like, how fun he was, what a great guy he was—and I feel so guilty."

Eric looked up at the ceiling. "Guilt won't bring him back." But he felt guilty himself. *What a rotten person I was—I am*, he thought.

He didn't remember Sean, wouldn't even know what he looked like had he not looked him up in the yearbook. But what Chris had just told him made him feel bad. Their best friend had been gay, and they'd just turned their backs on him, pretended like they hadn't known him.

"Who did Sean hang out with?" he asked.

"I never paid him much attention after that," Chris replied. "I don't know who he hung around with, who his friends were. I never saw him with anyone."

"Do you think—do you think maybe someone killed him because he was gay?" Eric shook his head. He couldn't wrap his mind around it. Even if that were true, how had Sean wound up in his car? "And you have no idea where I was, what I did, the day of the accident?"

Chris shook his head. "No, man, like I said, you hadn't talked to me since—well, since you know."

"He didn't go out for football or anything? What kind of activities was he involved in?"

"He was on the school paper, I think. At least he hung out with those kids." Chris shrugged. "I only looked at the paper when my picture was in it."

Eric leaned his head back on the pillows. He was tired, but his mind was still racing on. He yawned.

"Dude, you get some sleep." Chris stood up. "I have to work tomorrow, but I'll come by after I get off, is that cool?"

Eric nodded.

Chris started to reach his hand out for a shake, but thought better of it and pulled back. "All right, man." He stopped at the door. "I'm glad you're okay, man."

Eric just nodded. When the door closed, he opened the yearbook to the index. He looked up Sean, and left his hand there as he flipped through to find the pages listed behind Sean's name.

There were only three other pages besides Sean's class picture.

One was the newspaper staff. Eric studied their faces, read their names in the caption beneath the photograph. None of the names or faces meant anything to him—he hadn't thought they would.

The next page was the yearbook page. Sean apparently was one of the photographers. He turned back to the newspaper page—Sean was the only person on both pages.

The third page had a picture of Sean sitting under a tree looking at a laptop. There was a boy seated on either side of him, looking at the same thing and laughing.

One's name was Kerry Gargaro; the other was Bob Nowicki.

Both were also on the yearbook staff.

He flipped back to the index and found their class pictures. Their class pictures were both in the junior section—on the same page as Eric's.

Okay, Eric thought, closing the yearbook. *Kerry Gargaro and Bob Nowicki—that's where I'll start.*

He closed his eyes.

CHAPTER FIVE

W"ake up, honey."
Eric opened his eyes and yawned. His mother smiled down at him. "Go brush your teeth and wash your face, honey. Your father's home and I'm about to put dinner on the table. I made your favorite—Swedish meatballs."

He sat up and yawned, glancing at the clock on the bedside table. It was after six. The yearbook was lying on the bed next to him, open to the picture of Sean, Terry, and Bob. His mother gave it a glance before shutting it. With no expression, she picked the yearbook up and put it back on his desk. She gave him a funny look, and he dreaded what was coming next.

He was expecting her to ask about the picture. Instead, she said, "Trying to jog your memory?" Her face was sad, her lower lip trembling as if she were struggling to keep from crying. "It's okay, honey, it'll come back. I know it will. Dr. Weston said it was rarely permanent. I know it's hard, but you just have to be patient."

Feeling a little guilty, he just nodded.

"I'm so glad Chris came by," she went on. "He came by a lot when you were unconscious, you know. But he started working at the country club—and couldn't make it anymore during visiting hours after that."

"Yeah, that's what he said." Eric swung his legs to the floor and stood up, yawning and stretching until pain from his ribs jabbed him. He started to follow her out of the room, but detoured instead into the bathroom. He turned on the hot water and washed the sleep out of his eyes, staring at himself in the mirror. He'd lost about twenty pounds while in the hospital, Dr. Weston had told him before he checked out that morning, and his mother had commented more than once about needing to "put the weight back on him." He wasn't hungry—and before looking at the pictures on the living room wall and going through the yearbook, he hadn't known what she'd meant. But now, looking at himself in the mirror, he could see his face was a lot thinner than in the pictures. The shorts were baggy and too big in the waist—he had to keep hiking them up. He sighed and reached for a toothbrush—but stopped. He didn't know which was his, so he just rubbed toothpaste onto his index finger and ran it over his teeth.

When he got downstairs, he could hear voices in the kitchen, so he followed the sound, pushing his way through the saloon doors. Under a hanging chandelier, the table was set. Everything smelled good, and his stomach growled. His father and Danny were already seated, and his mother was placing glasses of milk at every setting. He slid into a seat and smiled at his father, ignoring Danny's scowl.

"Welcome home, Eric," his father said, smiling back at him. "How are you feeling? You glad to be here?"

"I feel okay, I guess." He shrugged. "And anything's better than the hospital."

His mother put a large bowl of Swedish meatballs in the center of the table, next to a large bowl of egg noodles. The aroma made his mouth water, and his stomach growled again.

His father took the bowl of noodles and helped himself before passing the bowl to him. Eric spooned himself a generous helping, and handed the bowl to Danny just in time to take the bowl of meatballs from his father. He covered the noodles with meatballs and gravy, and the smell triggered—

—he was sitting at the table, in the exact same setting—only his mother was dressed differently—she was wearing maroon sweats with Woodbridge State University *across her chest, and she was talking as she stirred the meatballs and gravy into the noodles already on her plate. "So I told her in no uncertain terms what I thought of her behavior, that it was completely unacceptable, and she owed everyone at the meeting an apology." She shook her head. "I just don't understand that woman." She made a face. "I mean, it's bad enough she owns a bar, but to try to disrupt the PTA meeting that way?" She glanced over at Eric before adding, "Not that there's anything wrong with that, of course. Gina Brody doesn't have much of a choice, I know, since her husband died, and she's doing the best she can. But I swear, since the boys aren't friends anymore, all she does is oppose me just because." She speared a meatball with her fork. "I bet if I made a motion to say that the sky is blue, she'd vote against it and swear the sky is green."*

"Well, Nancy, I'm proud you stood up for yourself," his father said with a smile. He was wearing different clothing too—a dark blue sweater over a white collared shirt with no tie. "How was practice today, Danny?"

Danny shrugged. "Same as always." He said it through a mouthful of meatballs.

"Don't talk with your mouth full," his mother snapped.

"Do you think you'll get to play any this season?"

"Don't know."

His father sighed and looked at Eric, a slightly exasperated expression on his face, which clearly read "I just don't know what to do with your brother."

Eric swallowed and said, "Danny, I can help you with your batting and fielding if you want."

"No thanks," Danny replied without looking up from his plate.

Eric felt his temper starting to rise. He glared across the table at his little brother, his mind filling with contempt. Look at him, he thought angrily, what a little slob he is. He doesn't care about anything, he doesn't care about the way he dresses or the way he looks, he just wants to sit around and whine about how unfair everything is—

—he jolted back into the present. Everyone was staring at him. "Are you feeling okay, Eric?" his mother said in a quiet, nervous voice.

"I'm—fine." He tried to give her a reassuring smile. His heart was pounding. *That was a memory,* he thought, searching through his mind, trying to grab hold of it and bring out the rest of it. Their words still rang in his ears. It had been so clear—it was like he'd been sitting at the table that night again. He glanced over at Danny, who was staring down at his plate—just like he had been in the memory—and he could remember the feeling of contempt he'd had that night with his brother. *Is that why Danny hates me?* he wondered as he put another spoonful of meatballs in his mouth and chewed. It disturbed him—the memory of the clear dislike he had for his brother before the accident.

"Mom, did you not like Sean's mother?" Eric asked.

There was a clatter as Mom dropped her fork back to her plate. She took a drink from her glass of milk, exchanging a glance with her husband, and set the glass back down. "Now, Eric, why would you ask that?" she asked in a calm, quiet voice.

"It's just—" He stopped himself, looking over at Danny out of the corner of his eyes. Danny was eating and not looking up. "I just had a feeling about it."

"I like Gina Brody just fine," she replied with a bright smile. "We've had some disagreements over PTA business, but she's a very nice woman."

"She's telling everyone in town you killed her son," Danny said without looking up. "And she's also telling everyone Uncle Arnie is stalling the investigation because you're his nephew."

"Danny!" Mom said sharply. She took a deep breath.

"Is that true?" Eric asked. He picked up a meatball and a spoonful of noodles.

"Mrs. Brody is just upset, son," Dad replied. "She lost her son, and she wants answers. I'd feel the same if I were in her situation. But your uncle is doing the best he can—I don't think anyone could do a better job, given the circumstances."

"My amnesia, you mean." Eric took another bite.

"Yes, that's right. Until your memory comes back, there really isn't much your uncle can do. He doesn't even know where Sean was shot, where you were coming back from." His father patted the sides of his mouth with his napkin. "Oh, and Eric, I have your laptop," his father said. "Your uncle brought it by my office this afternoon."

"It's about time," Mom said. "They didn't need to keep it all this time."

"I didn't even know he had it," Eric said slowly. His mother had brought the laptop to the hospital, but he'd never used it. He hadn't noticed that it was gone. "Why did he take it?"

"It's apparently routine," his father replied. His voice was even, his face without expression. "I did make them get a warrant, though. They were looking for, um, evidence. Apparently they didn't find any."

"Of course they didn't find anything because there was nothing to find. I've told Arnie that until I am blue in the face." Mom's voice was tight and angry. "How many times do I have to tell them Eric couldn't have—couldn't have…" Her voice trailed off for a moment, and then she added, "done what they think he did."

"It's okay, Mom, you can say it." Eric watched Danny shifting uncomfortably in his seat. "They think I killed Sean Brody."

"Don't you ever say that!" she snapped, her fork clanking against the plate in front of her. "Never say that! It isn't true."

Danny's face reddened, but he didn't say anything. He just kept eating.

"It's what they think, Mom." Eric shrugged. "Not saying it isn't going to change it."

Her mouth opened and closed without making a sound, before she turned her attention back to her plate.

"There's something else, too." Now it was Dad's turn to shift uncomfortably in his seat. "The police want one of their psychiatrists to talk to Eric—"

"Absolutely not!" Mom snapped. "I won't allow it!"

Dad took a deep breath. "Melanie, the more we try to hinder the investigation, the more it looks like we have something to hide. I told him to have the psychiatrist come over tomorrow morning and Eric would talk with her. Her name is Guzman, I think he said." He smiled at Eric. "She's apparently one of the best in the field. She drove up from Sacramento just to talk to you."

Her voice rose with hysteria. "They're hounding him, Nick! And I won't have my son railroaded! He didn't do anything wrong!"

He took a deep breath. "Melanie, I met with her. I don't think she's going to try to railroad him. She's a professional. All she can tell the police is her opinion about his mental state, whether or not he has amnesia. She can't tell them anything he says—that would be a violation of her professional ethics."

"I don't like it, I don't like it one bit." Mom tossed her fork down onto her plate. "Maybe we need to get him a lawyer, Nick. I don't like this. I don't like this at all."

"Danny's right, Mel. There's already enough talk around town that Arnie is not"—he hesitated—"pushing this investigation because his nephew is a suspect. If we get him a lawyer, if we don't let him meet with Dr. Guzman, how is that going to look? You've seen the garbage they've been putting in the paper—"

"What have they been putting in the paper?" Eric interrupted. He could feel a slight pain starting behind his right eye—the side of his head where the concussion was located. *I haven't even seen a newspaper since before*, he thought. "What are they saying?"

"Lies," Mom snapped. "Nothing but lies. I'm going to cancel our subscription—"

"You'll do no such thing." Dad interrupted her. "If it wasn't Eric, Melanie, we'd be thinking the same thing. We need to be as cooperative as possible." Dad went on, like Eric hadn't said a word, "We can't give the impression that—"

Danny interrupted in a nasty tone. "They're saying you killed Sean, and Uncle Arnie is blocking the investigation, that you're faking the amnesia and he's going along with it to protect you from paying for your crime." His eyes were narrowed to slits, glaring at Eric. "It's easy for you, Eric. You're in the hospital for weeks, and now here in the house, not going anywhere, not seeing anyone. You're not the one who has to go out in public every day and listen to all the people whispering and pointing." He threw his spoon down, and it bounced off the table, clattering on the floor. His face reddened, his voice shaking, hands trembling as he pushed himself to his feet. "My best friend's parents told him he couldn't hang around with me anymore." His voice rose. "Are you happy now? You've *ruined* my life! Murderer!"

"Danny! You apologize to your brother right now!" Mom's face turned the exact same shade of red as Danny's.

"I *won't*!" Danny shouted. "I'm not going to baseball practice anymore either! The last game was HORRIBLE! Everyone was pointing and staring and nobody will talk to me anymore and I WON'T DO IT!"

Mom moved quickly around the table and the sound of a slap echoed in the room.

As soon as she did it, her other hand flew to her mouth. "Danny, I'm sorry—"

He ran out of the room. They could hear his feet stomping up the stairs, and a few moments later a door slammed shut.

Mom looked stricken. Her eyes filled with tears, she looked at Eric. "I'm sorry," she half whispered. "I—"

She turned and ran out of the room.

"This is my fault," Eric said, staring down at his plate. He felt sick to his stomach. "Dad, I'm so sorry."

"It's not your fault, Eric. Don't blame yourself because a lot of people in this town are small-minded." He forced a smile that didn't quite reach his eyes. He got up and poured himself a glass of whiskey. He wouldn't meet Eric's eyes, just stared down into the brown liquid in the glass. "We've been so focused on ourselves—and you—I've not given your brother a thought." He shook his head. "I can't imagine how hard this has been on him."

"I'm sorry." Eric bit his lower lip, struggling to keep tears down. "I hate this, Dad." He slammed his fists down on the table. "Why can't I remember anything? *Why is this happening to me?*"

"I wish I could answer that, son." Dad sank back down

into his chair heavily. "Bad things happen to good people, that's just the way of the world, Eric. It's always been that way and it doesn't look like it's going to change any time soon."

"Dad, was I a good person?" Eric pushed his plate away. He'd only eaten half of his food but his appetite was gone. It didn't smell good to him anymore. "I don't even know that."

"You *are* a good person," Dad replied. "You're kind and thoughtful, you're a good student. You've never given your mother and me a moment's worry. Don't ever think otherwise."

Well, of course he's going to say that—he's my father and he loves me. Eric shook his head. "I don't know. Danny doesn't seem to like me very much—my own brother. And if people seem to think I was capable of"—he couldn't bring himself to say the words—"what they think I did, then how could I have been a good person, Dad?"

"The world is a very strange place." His father reached over and touched Eric's arm. "You were—*are*—the Big Man on Campus at Woodbridge High. You were Homecoming royalty last year, you've already been voted captain of the football team for next year, you were the big star on the football team and you were one of the best hitters on the baseball team this past spring. People—people always like boys like you. But they turn really quickly when something bad happens. I don't understand it—it's a part of human nature I just don't get. But there you have it; that's how it is. People always like to build someone up just so they can tear them down again. But don't you worry—there are a lot of small-minded people, but there's also a lot of good people out there—people who don't believe you could have killed Sean." He sighed. "And no matter how much your mother wants to blame Sean's mother for all of this, Mrs. Brody should be pitied. No matter what she says, we should feel bad for her. She lost her son—we still have ours. And I can't even begin to imagine what she must be going through." He took another drink of the whiskey. "So, that's why I think you should talk to Dr. Guzman, Eric. Mrs. Brody deserves to know what happened, she deserves answers. I don't think you're faking—you wouldn't ever do something like that. You've always taken responsibility for your mistakes, for your actions. I don't believe you'd change that way."

Eric felt a sob coming up in his throat, and took his father's hand—

—and once again, felt that weird sensation, like an electric shock, go up his arm.

My God, will this nightmare ever end? My poor son, I can't imagine what you must be going through. I just hope and pray this doctor will be able to make some progress with you, help your memory come back. If you did kill Sean, you can atone for it. I know you will do the right thing. We raised you to and you always have, but if you didn't kill him, everyone needs to know. If they don't ever find out who actually did kill Sean, this is going to haunt you for the rest of your life, because there will always be people who will think you got away with murder. I don't want that to follow you around the rest of your life, so we've got to get to the bottom of this before—

His father's face had gone pale. He pulled his hand away, rubbing it with the other. "What—what was *that*?" He forced a laugh. "That was a hell of an electric shock!" He kept rubbing his hand.

Eric stared at him, swallowing hard. *How do I explain this to my father? How do I explain this to anyone?* He didn't know what to say, how to try to start explaining something he didn't even fully understand himself. He opened and closed his mouth.

He was saved by the reappearance of his mother and brother. Their eyes were red—obviously they had been crying. Danny slid back down into his seat without looking at him. He looked down at his dinner plate. "I'm sorry, Eric, I didn't mean it," he mumbled.

Mom sat down in her chair, her eyebrows raising as she looked at Eric expectantly, waiting for him to say something.

"I'm sorry, too, Danny." Eric replied. He pushed his chair back from the table. "I'm not hungry anymore. I think I need some fresh air. I think I'll take a walk."

No one said anything as he opened the back door and walked outside.

The night was cool, and a breeze was blowing down from the mountain. He stood there for a moment on the back steps, looking up at the stars. They looked close enough to reach up and grab. *How could I forget how beautiful the night sky is?* he wondered as he stepped down into the grass. He heard the sound of laughter from a few houses away, and could smell charcoal smoke. A car drove by on the street out front. He could hear crickets chirping, and in the woods behind the house an owl hooted.

He smiled, breathing in the deep scent of pine in the cool air. *It does feel good to be out of the hospital*, he thought.

He walked across the backyard, looking around. A swing-set stood in a corner of the yard, and there was a sandbox just in front of it. A fountain bubbled in the center of the backyard, and there was a picnic table right next to it. On the other side of the picnic table was a brick barbecue pit. He looked up and saw the lights of an airplane speeding across the sky far above. He kept walking and opened the back gate. It was darker out in the woods than in the yard, and he took a tentative step forward. It seemed vaguely familiar, but when he tried to grab on to the memory it disappeared. He sighed.

There was a path leading from the gate into the woods, and he followed it. He heard Chris saying *We camped out in the woods behind your house.* So, the place where they used to camp was probably along the path somewhere. The ground sloped up, and he kept walking, following the path. Overhead the stars blinked down on him. It *did* seem familiar, he realized. He stopped and stared at a pine tree when the path curved to the left. He walked over and put his hand on it, about shoulder level, and with his fingers traced the letters *EM + LT*, encircled by a heart. *I must have carved that,* he thought, *and I knew somehow it was there.*

He turned back to the path when he heard a twig snap nearby.

He froze, barely able to breathe, listening for another sound.

He was just about to dismiss it as his imagination when there was a loud bang.

Something whistled past his head.

His heart leaped into his throat.

Someone just shot at me!

He turned and ran back down the path, and as he ran—

—it became broad daylight and he was looking down at Sean. Blood was pumping out of his chest. His eyes were wide, his mouth moving but no sound was coming out. "Oh my God!" He knelt down beside Sean, and felt something cut his left knee. He glanced around and saw nothing but trees.

"Please," Sean gasped out. "Get out of here. You need to get out of here."

But he knew he couldn't do that.

And he scooped Sean up in his arms without hesitating. He turned and ran with him over to where his car was parked, and somehow got the back door open. He put Sean down in the backseat and ran around to the driver's side. He opened the door, fumbling with the keys because his hands were shaking. But he finally managed to get the ignition key inserted. He turned it and slammed the car into reverse. A cloud of dust flew up as he shoved the gearshift over to D and floored the accelerator. The car jumped forward along the dirt road, climbing steadily until he could see the county road ahead. "Hang in there, Sean!" he shouted—

—and he was opening the back gate. He slammed it shut behind him, panting. Through the kitchen windows, he could see his family eating. He leaned against the gate, panting, trying to get his breathing under control.

I'm starting to remember, he thought as his heart rate slowed.

Someone shot at me in the woods.

But now, safely back inside the fence, he wasn't so sure he hadn't imagined it.

He took a deep breath and walked across the yard to the back door.

CHAPTER SIX

He didn't sleep well.

It took him a long time to fall asleep—his own bed was so much more comfortable than the hospital bed, and the absolute silence inside the house just didn't feel right. *I've gotten used to the hospital noise,* he thought after he turned over for what seemed like the thousandth time. He debated taking a sleeping pill—his nightstand drawer looked like a pharmacy shelf—but decided not to. *I need to stop taking pills and adjust to normal life—or what passes for normal when you can't remember anything.*

He finally fell asleep but kept having the same dream over and over—Sean standing in front of him, the sound of the shot, the look on his face as he went down—and would wake up, his heart pounding and gasping for breath.

At four in the morning, he woke up again. He stared at the ceiling in the darkness. *Take a sleeping pill,* a voice whispered in his head, *just this once, what's it going to hurt?*

He turned on the lamp on his nightstand and had his hand on the bottle when he stopped himself. *If I take one now I'll sleep till noon.*

He put the bottle back. He slid out of the bed and went into the bathroom for a glass of water. He stared at himself in the mirror. His eyes were red and swollen. His hand shook slightly as he raised the glass to his mouth to drink. He took a big swallow, closed his eyes, and took some deep breaths.

I'm starting to remember things—this is good, he reminded himself. *And I didn't shoot Sean—I couldn't have. If the memory is right—and why wouldn't it be—I didn't have a gun and I didn't want him dead. Someone else did.*

But who did—and why? What could he have done that would make someone want to kill him? He was a high school student—none of this makes any sense. But he is dead. Someone did shoot him.

He splashed some cold water onto his face and smiled at his reflection. *Maybe my whole memory will be back in a few days and this nightmare will be over*, he reassured himself. He turned off the bathroom light.

He got back into bed and pulled the covers up to his chin. The bed was so comfortable, and the blankets felt good and warm. The house was cold—he could hear the air-conditioning coming through the vent in the ceiling—and he shivered a bit as he rolled onto his back.

He lay there in the dark, staring at the ceiling, his mind racing.

Chris said Sean was gay and that was why we stopped being friends with him. Maybe that was why someone killed him? But does that make sense? Surely no one would kill someone over that, would they?

But it was enough reason for you to not want to be friends with him. Why? What difference did it make? He was the same person, wasn't he?

He felt himself drifting off to sleep again, and he turned onto his side. *In the morning*, he decided, *I'll figure out what to do next...*

Eric sat up in bed with a jolt, gasping for breath. He could hear his heart pounding. He leaned back against the headboard as the terror from the dream faded away. He shook his head and rubbed the sleep out of his eyes.

Bright sunlight was coming through the windows. The clock on the nightstand read 9:30.

As awful as it had been, he tried to remember the dream.

It was different from the ones that kept waking him up all night, that much he remembered, and he couldn't shake the feeling that it had been important. *It might have been a memory rather than a dream*, he reminded himself. *Try to remember it.* He closed his eyes and mentally reached for the disappearing tendrils. But it was fading away, no matter how hard he tried.

And then it was completely gone.

All he could remember was he'd been out there in the country in that same place as before, and Sean had been there, too. But this time, Sean had told him—

What did Sean tell me?

He felt like screaming. He slammed his hands down on the bed in frustration. It was *important*, but whatever it was, it was gone. He swore under his breath. "Maybe it wasn't a memory," he reassured himself as he got out of the bed, "it could have just been a dream."

But he didn't believe it, no matter how much he wanted to.

He yawned and stretched—and a sharp jab of pain from his ribs doubled him over almost immediately, like his ribs whispered, *Remember me?* His pain pills were sitting on the nightstand, and he started reaching for them—but pulled back just as his hand was about to close around the bottle. *I need my head to be clear*, he reminded himself, *if I'm going to figure out what happened out there in the country. The pain isn't that bad—it's nothing I haven't handled before in a football game.*

As soon as he thought the words he had a flash.

He was standing behind the quarterback, who was calling out signals. It was a night game and the stadium lights were on. It was chilly as he waited for the snap count. He could hear the crowd chanting, "Touchdown! Touchdown!" He glanced over to the sideline out of the corner of his eye. Coach Walton was standing there, his arms folded, his eyes narrowed in concentration, his jaw set. Eric knew that look.

He glanced up at the scoreboard. Visitors 20, Home 16. The game clock read 2:03, and the little green light under the 4 was lit. Fourth quarter, undefeated streak and the conference title on the line—they needed to score. It was 3rd and long, and they were on the 23 yard line. There was still time to get a first down and try for the touchdown. His heart was in his throat. He could see the linebackers on the other side staring at him.

They'd been keying on him all night, and he hadn't gotten as much yardage as he usually did. He hadn't even scored—they'd scored their two touchdowns on a pass to the wide receiver and on a long run by Chris. This was the first game all season where he hadn't scored. And he was getting the ball this time. He had to make eight yards at least.

He'd run the ball on first down and been stopped at the line of scrimmage.

He looked over at the sideline. He could see Lacey. She and the other cheerleaders had their backs to the crowd, but they were still leading the chant.

"Hut One! Hut Two!"

And the ball was snapped and he started running forward. The quarterback—Kerry Malloy, that was his name—turned and shoved the football into his stomach just as the left tackle created an opening for him to run through—and he could see all the way to the goal line. He closed his hands over the ball and started accelerating.

He could hear the crowd screaming as he ran. He straight-armed the linebacker bearing down on him and broke free. Out of the corner of his eye he saw the wide receiver take the safety out.

It was clear sailing.

He put his head down and ran, cheers echoing in the stadium.

He was at the ten, the nine, eight, five.

He was almost to the goal line when he was slammed from both sides, and he held on to the football for dear life as stars started dancing in front of his eyes and everything started going black. He started to go down, oh so close to the goal line, and as the world went crazy and his vision blurred he knew all he had to do was just hold on to the ball and fall forward and he would cross the goal line and the game would be won...

"The game against Oakhurst," he said out loud, a slight smile playing at his lips. He'd scored, all right, even though he'd been knocked out. He'd had to come out of the game to take a breather, and Chris had punched the ball in for the two-point conversion to put them up 24–20. He'd watched from the sidelines as the defense held and time ran out.

And when the gun went off signaling the win, the crowd had poured out onto the field cheering and screaming.

Lacey had found him, thrown her arms around him, and they'd kissed.

Finally, a good memory, he thought.

His memory might only be coming back in bits and pieces, but it was definitely starting to come back. And that was progress, like Dr. Weston had said. Every little memory was a piece of the big puzzle snapping back into place.

And before I know it, I'll remember everything.

He put the pill bottle back into the nightstand drawer and, wincing, walked over to the window and looked out.

His mother, in a T-shirt and shorts, her head covered by a huge floppy hat, was pulling weeds with a trowel from the lawn. She stopped for a moment and wiped at her forehead. There was a circle of sweat in the center of her back. She took a drink out of a bottle of water before starting to work on another weed.

She's my mother and I still don't feel anything when I look at her. But I will, I know I will.

He watched her for a moment before going into the bathroom to wash his face and brush his teeth. He rinsed his mouth and smiled at himself in the mirror. He felt better than he had since waking up in the hospital. *You're starting to remember things*—he winked at his reflection—*and you didn't kill Sean. That's the most important thing, that's why you feel better about everything.*

And if you can remember that—and a play in a football game, and a dinner sometime in the past, well, your memory is on its way back. It's just a matter of time.

He felt happier than he could remember feeling.

So, what else might trigger some memories? He looked at his desk. His laptop was sitting there, closed. There was a WHS decal on its sleek silver top. He walked over to his desk and sat down.

He ran his hands along the edges of the little computer—and rolled his eyes. *Touching your computer isn't going to do anything, dumbass*, he scolded himself, opening the laptop. He pressed the power button, and while it booted up, he flipped through the pages of his yearbook again. He paused at the picture of the junior class officers.

We look so happy, he thought, *not a care in the world.*

He stared at the picture. *You'd have never thought in a million years that she would sleep with Chris*, he thought.

There was a slight glimmer of emotion, and then—

"I'm so sorry." Lacey was crying, wiping at her eyes. *She*

was wearing a Lady Gaga T-shirt and a pair of khaki shorts. It was sunny, and they were sitting at a picnic table—a park he didn't recognize. He could hear kids playing, cars driving by. "You know I love you, Eric."

It hurt—it felt like he was being stabbed repeatedly in the heart. He couldn't believe she did this to him. She was supposed to LOVE me, he thought, and Chris has been my best friend, like a brother, to me my WHOLE FRIGGING LIFE and all it takes is a couple of beers? And they're doing this? What kind of people are they?

He stood up. "I will never speak to you again," he said, his voice sounding distant, stronger than he felt inside. Inside he was dying, falling apart, wanting to scream and cry and punch something.

"Eric, please!"

"We're done."

He left her sitting at the picnic table and walked to his car, never looking back, not even when he got into the car and drove away.

As he drove, the anger gave way to sadness. He blinked away tears. Crying's not going to do me any good, he told himself, trying to summon up the anger again. But it wouldn't come, he was overwhelmed with grief. What did I ever do to deserve this? he asked himself as he stopped at a red light.

As if in answer to his question, a bicycle went through the intersection in front of him. It was Sean Brody. He was wearing a Fresno State tank top and a pair of jean shorts, and a Fresno State baseball cap. He didn't look in Eric's direction.

Eric watched him pedal away. That's what you did to deserve this, a voice whispered in the back of his mind, think about the way you treated him, you were friends ever since you were kids and you turned your back on him and made his life miserable.

Now you know how it feels to have a friend turn on you, stab you in the back for no reason—you're getting exactly what you deserve.

A car honked behind him. The light had turned green. He shook his head and drove through the intersection.

I need to make it up to Sean, he told himself. I need to apologize.

And then an image of Chris and Lacey flashed through his mind—

He gasped and leaned back in his desk chair with his eyes closed.

The agony was worse than his ribs, worse than when the pain killers wore off in the hospital. He took a few deep breaths. It felt like his heart was being torn out of his chest all over again, and tears rose in his eyes. His mind felt like it was melting down.

And then it was gone, like it never happened.

He shook his head. "My girlfriend and my best friend slept together," he said out loud. He felt nothing.

Nothing but an emptiness inside that was worse than the pain.

He opened his eyes and stared at his computer screen, closing the yearbook and putting it aside. There was only one folder on his desktop, labeled *my stuff*. He clicked it open, and a huge directory scrolled up. The file names meant nothing to him. He opened a few of them—one was a term paper for a Mr. Driscoll's history class. He'd written about the Battle of Antietam Creek. He closed them and clicked on the folder marked *Pictures*.

He sighed. There were several hundred pictures in the file, none of them labeled. He clicked on one. It was of him and Chris. They both were only wearing shorts that reached their knees, and they were soaking wet. Their wet hair was plastered to their heads, and both were grinning stupidly at the camera. They were both holding up cans of beer as though toasting the person taking the picture.

He looked closer. They were standing beside a clear creek on dark yellow sand. Pine trees stood on the other side of the narrow creek, and just to their left was an incline of dirt. There was a Styrofoam cooler just behind them, with its lid off. He could see ice and more beer cans inside. The sun was pretty bright, but it was behind the camera—their shadows extended out behind them.

He clicked on the next picture—this one was of him with Lacey, standing in almost the exact same spot. Lacey was wearing a hot pink bikini, her hair pulled back into a ponytail. She was standing in the water, which reached her ankles. His right arm was around her waist, and he was looking at her with a big smile on his face. She was smiling at the camera, not looking at him.

The next picture was of Chris, with his back to the incline. He was wearing sunglasses, and had his tongue out. He was making a rather bizarre face. Whoever had taken the picture must have been sitting down, because the perspective made Chris look like a giant. The incline rose high behind him.

The Ledge, he thought.

He closed his eyes and tried to pursue the thought, but it was gone. But he knew he was right—these pictures were taken at a place they called the Ledge.

But he had no idea where it was.

He could feel the frustration rising, and he fought it down.

Lacey, he thought, *she'd know.*

He pulled out a pad of paper from his desk drawer and wrote *The Ledge* across the top of the page. Underneath it, he added Chris's and Lacey's names.

He started clicking through the pictures. There were about twenty more taken along the shore of the creek—Lacey lying down across a blanket, he and Chris splashing each other in the water—but there was nothing in any of them that triggered another memory, or told him something he hadn't already figured out.

The next group of pictures—thirty or so—were from a bowling alley. The majority were again of the three of them. Occasionally there was another kid in one of the pictures—some who'd visited him in the hospital—but again, they triggered nothing.

How come Chris never has a girlfriend?

He scrolled through the pictures again, trying to see if there were any girls who seemed like Chris's girlfriend in any of them.

There wasn't a single picture where Chris had his arm around a girl who wasn't Lacey. No pictures where he was holding hands with a girl.

Had he always been after Lacey? Was there more to what happened at that party than either one of them was letting on?

"It's not like I can remember," he murmured. He scratched his head. He wrote *Chris + Lacey* on the notepad with a question mark after their names.

After another few minutes he closed the folder.

He clicked on the blue lowercase *e* and the Internet browser loaded. Just like when he'd checked it in the hospital, when it finished loading it took him to his Facebook page.

Unlike when he'd checked it at the hospital, this time the login name was filled in: ericmatthews4@woodbridgehs.com.

And the box for the password was filled in with seven black dots.

He bit his lower lip and clicked on the Log In box.

The page reloaded.

The front page was covered with get well wishes from

people whose names he didn't recognize. On the left sidebar, he saw that he had 137 friends.

There was an 11 in red underneath the message icon. He clicked on it.

The messages loaded, and he froze.

The last one marked Read was from Sean Brody. It was dated the day of the accident.

There was no subject line.

He pushed his chair back and swallowed.

You have to read it.

He clicked on the message.

Eric:

> *I can't go on this way anymore. This has to stop. I can't live like this. Please meet me at the Ledge tomorrow at eleven. Please?*
>
> *Sean*

The Ledge.

"What was going on, Sean?" he said out loud, staring at the message. "If we weren't friends, what did you want from me?"

His computer beeped. A little window had opened in the lower right corner of the main window.

LACEY TREMAYNE: Hi, Eric. How are you feeling?

He typed: Okay, I guess. A little confused.

LACEY TREMAYNE: This must be so hard on you.

ERIC MATTHEWS: It'll get easier I suppose.

LACEY TREMAYNE: I wish there was something I could do.

ERIC MATTHEWS: Can you come over? I want to talk to you about something.

LACEY TREMAYNE: I can't right now, but in a couple of hours I can is that okay?
ERIC MATTHEWS: Yes, that would be great. Thanks.

He looked over at the left side of the screen. He clicked on the Friends link and started scrolling through the names and faces.

Neither Bob Nowicki nor Kerry Gargaro were listed as his friends.

No surprise there, he thought. Sean wasn't listed as one of his friends, either.

He did a search on the site for Bob Nowicki and found his page. All information was restricted to Friends Only, but the picture was definitely the same kid from the yearbook picture.

He clicked on the message symbol, and typed:

> *Bob:*
> *I need to talk to both you and Kerry. Please. I need your help.*
> *Eric*

Almost immediately, his computer dinged. Bob had answered.

He clicked it open.

> *Eric:*
> *Why on earth would I want to help you? You killed my best friend. Everyone knows the only reason you aren't in jail is because your uncle is the sheriff. Go to hell, murderer.*

There it was, in black and white. He felt like he'd been

punched in the stomach. He gritted his teeth. "Well, what did you expect?" he asked himself out loud. He pushed back from the desk and walked over to the window.

Danny was right.

People thought he'd killed Sean.

He looked out the window and wiped at his eyes.

Why is this happening to me? What did I do?

"You didn't kill him," he said out loud. He repeated it several times.

He closed his eyes and concentrated.

The memory was still there. Sean standing in front of him, the sound of the shot, the look of surprise on Sean's face as he went down.

"You tried to save him," he whispered as he remembered somehow picking Sean up and running to the car, putting him in the backseat, the gurgling noises as he started the car and drove up the dirt road—

— but just like before, once the car reached the paved road, everything went gray.

But could he convince Bob and Kerry he'd tried to save Sean?

Could he convince *anyone*?

A car turned into the driveway, a red Mercedes. His mother got up from the flower bed and wiped her hands off on her shorts. The car door opened and a woman got out. She was wearing black slacks and a matching blazer over a red silk blouse. Her hair was pulled back from her face. She walked across the lawn, holding out her right hand to his mother. They shook hands and talked for a moment before turning and walking toward the house.

She must be the police psychologist, he thought. He walked back over to the computer and sat down.

He typed a response to Bob:

I don't blame you for hating me. I don't remember what happened. I'm trying to, and I think you and Kerry might be able to help me. I promise you—

He paused, closing his eyes.

—if you help me, and my memory comes back and I did kill him, I will confess.

He clicked Send, and once it was gone he scrolled through the other messages in his inbox. Several were from Lacey, one from Chris. He read them, and sighed. They were pretty much all the same—*I'm sorry can we please talk?*

There was a glimmer inside his mind, something trying to force its way into his consciousness, but when he tried, it went away.

He closed the laptop. Maybe Bob wouldn't talk to him, but he had at least made an effort.

I'll bet he'll talk to Lacey, he thought, and smiled. *I'll ask her to talk to him, convince him to meet me.*

A knock on his door startled him out of his thoughts. "Yes?" he called out.

His mother stuck her head in the door. "The police psychologist is here." Her face was sad, and she was wringing her hands. "Should I send her up?"

He nodded, giving her a shaky smile. "Thanks, Mom."

Chapter Seven

Eric got up from his desk and sat on the edge of the bed. He tried to calm his nerves.

She works for the police. She's going to try to get you to admit you killed Sean.

He shook his head. That didn't make sense—he was just being paranoid.

Besides, he reminded himself, *now you know you didn't shoot him. You just don't know who did.*

It wasn't a very reassuring thought.

"I'm not going to lie," he decided. "I'm going to tell her the truth. If she doesn't believe me, there's nothing I can do about it."

And didn't his parents always tell him that telling the truth was always the best way to go?

No matter what this woman thought—or his uncle, or anyone else in town, for that matter—he *knew* he wasn't a murderer. He'd tried to *save* Sean.

He remembered very clearly the emotions he'd felt as Sean lay there. Shock mostly, and horror—but also the need to get him help right away.

If I wanted him dead—if I'd shot him—I would have just left him there to die. I didn't do that. I carried him to the car and tried to get him to the hospital. That isn't what a murderer would do.

At least, he didn't think so.

And it was Sean's idea to meet out there, not mine. I didn't lure him to the Ledge so I could shoot him.

His eyes widened. *Who else knew we were going out there? Did I tell someone—or did Sean?*

It was even more important now to talk to Bob and Kerry.

He licked his lips. *If someone else shot Sean, I might know who it was—*

A chill went through him. *And I might remember. And if I remember, that person is going to go to jail. Which would mean the killer would need to get rid of me, too.*

He remembered the feel of something passing close to his head in the woods, the sound of the gunshot. He shuddered. *Had someone tried to kill him?*

You should have said something to Mom and Dad last night, he berated himself, *even if you weren't sure someone was shooting at you. It might have been nothing, but you should have told them.*

He closed his eyes and retraced everything from the moment he'd walked out the back gate until he heard the shot.

It was definitely a shot.

He shivered.

Someone shot at me. That WAS a gunshot I heard. There was someone out there in the woods with me, and whoever it was wanted to hurt me—and the only reason someone would want to was because—because they were afraid I'd remember something about that day at the Ledge. It had to be whoever killed Sean.

He shook his head. *You're overreacting. Even if it was a gunshot, it doesn't mean someone was shooting at you. How would the killer know you were going to go out there? They couldn't have. So you're assuming that someone just sat out there all night on the off chance you'd go for a walk after dinner. It's a forest. Someone could have been shooting at a wolf or a coyote or a raccoon or something. It could have been some kid horsing around and didn't even know you were around. That's all it probably was. It might not have even been a gunshot.*

Then what did you feel buzz by your head?

He pushed those thoughts out of his head. *But the most important thing is you know you didn't shoot Sean—but you also don't know who did.*

But the killer didn't know that.

He was a threat to the killer.

And the killer has to get rid of me before my memory comes back.

He swallowed and leaned back against the wall. His heart was racing, and his head was starting to hurt a little bit. *Calm down, getting worked up over this isn't going to change anything. You need to talk to Uncle Arnie.*

But would Uncle Arnie take him at his word?

He took a couple of deep breaths to try to calm down. The police psychologist was going to be knocking on his door at any moment—and it wouldn't do him any good to seem agitated or afraid.

"Tell her the truth," he said to himself. "You have to. She might be able to help."

A few moments later there was a light knock on his door. Before he could say anything, it opened. She looked to be in her mid to late thirties. She pushed her glasses up her nose and gave him a tentative smile. "Good morning, Eric, I'm Dr. Guzman," she said, her head tilted to one side. "May I come in?"

He sat up in bed and smiled back at her. "Sure," he replied with a shrug, "thanks for coming here. I mean, I would have come down to the police station."

Her smile didn't waver as she walked in. She was reasonably attractive, he decided. Her thick black hair was pulled back away from her face, and as she pulled out his desk chair he saw the thick braid that fell down her back. She wore a pair of black slacks with a matching jacket over a dark red silk blouse. She was on the short side, maybe five-three, with a slender figure. He noticed her white Reebok running shoes as she turned the chair around to face his bed before sitting down.

"I thought it would be best for you to be in an environment you're comfortable in for our talk," she said, putting her purse down on the floor next to her feet. She gave him a reassuring smile. "The police station can be a little intimidating, and I want you to be as relaxed as possible. I want you to understand that I'm not here as an enemy," she went on. "I'm here to assess your mental state, and that's all. I'm not here to try to trick or trap you."

"You want to know if I'm faking or not," he said. "It's all right, Dr. Guzman. You're just doing your job." He smiled at her. "I'm just going to tell you the truth."

"I don't know that I would describe the purpose of my visit quite that harshly." She frowned, her forehead wrinkling and her eyesbrows knitting together. "Like I said, I'm not your enemy, Eric. My goal here is to help you." Her face relaxed. "If you'll let me."

"But you're here to figure out if I'm faking the amnesia, aren't you?" Eric shrugged. "It's okay. I get it."

"It's true that I'm here to assess your condition for the police, yes, I won't deny that." She took a deep breath. "But, Eric, your well-being is my primary concern. I want to make sure you know that, okay? I have an ethical duty as a doctor to put what's best for you ahead of what's best for the police. I'm on your side." She tilted her head to one side again. "And I'm ethically bound to keep anything you tell me confidential. I can't tell anyone what you say to me. Not your parents, not the police, no one. All I can tell the police is my assessment of your mental state."

"Even if I told you—" He stopped himself.

"Even if you told me you did kill Sean Brody, yes." She nodded. "Please understand, Eric, I *am* on your side." She crossed her right leg over her left. "Now, you've been through an incredibly traumatic experience. How do you feel about that?"

"Well, I don't really feel anything." He shrugged again. "It's frustrating to not be able to remember. But I'm starting to get, I don't know—flashes of memory." He leaned forward. "I *want* to remember, but it's just little bits and pieces, here and there. It drives me crazy—it's so frustrating." He pounded his fists onto the bed. "Like last night at dinner—my mom made Swedish meatballs because it was my favorite. While we were sitting there at the table I remembered another time she made them—we were all in the same chairs, the meal was exactly the same—but I don't know when it was. I remembered a little piece of the conversation—nothing important—and then just like that it was gone." He gave her a little smile. "But I still have that memory. What happened before and after that little bit, I have no idea."

"But that's encouraging, Eric." She beamed at him. "Your memory is coming back—even if it's just a little at a time. Have you had more of these? Besides the dinner?"

Can I really trust her? he wondered, biting his lip. He nodded.

"Do you want to tell me about it?"

The truth is always better than a lie. "I—I remember Sean being shot."

Her face didn't change expression. She just leaned forward a bit. "Okay, go on. What do you remember?"

"I didn't shoot him." He looked her right in the eyes. "I couldn't have. He was standing in front of me—maybe a couple of feet away? And I heard the gunshot—it was behind me. I saw him—" He closed his eyes. "I saw the look on his face. I saw him fall down. I remember feeling—scared and numb at the same time. He said something, I don't remember what he said, but I picked him up and carried him to the car. I remember thinking I had to get him to the hospital, he needed help and—" He swallowed. "I got his blood all over me." He looked at her. "I remember driving up the dirt road and getting to the paved one. That's where the memory stops." He realized he was clutching his blanket, twisting it in his hands, and let go of it. "I *remember* how I felt when it happened. I was horrified, Dr, Guzman. I was scared. I had to get him to the hospital. I had to get him help. Would I have done that if I shot him?"

Dr. Guzman's face remained impassive. "I don't know, Eric. Only you know that. You don't remember pulling the trigger?"

"No. I didn't have a gun, Dr. Guzman, so I couldn't have done it." He shook his head. "I don't even know why we were out there at the Ledge." He stopped himself before he mentioned the Facebook message.

Her eyebrows knit together. "The Ledge? Where's that?"

"I remember that's where we were. I don't know where it is." He looked at her again, watching her face. "I think it's out in the country somewhere. I found some pictures on my computer. The folder was called Ledge Pics or something like that. I'm pretty sure that's where we were."

"Do you want to remember?"

"Of course I want to remember!" he shot back. "You think I like not knowing who I am? You think I like looking at my parents and not feeling anything?"

"You don't feel anything when you look at your parents?" Her face was without expression, and her voice was level. She could have just as easily been asking about the weather.

He could feel frustration building inside, and he bit his lower lip, counting slowly to ten before he answered her through clenched teeth. "That's what I just said."

"You're getting angry." Her own voice remained level, emotionless. "I'm on your side, Eric, remember? We're just having a little chat, that's all."

"Nobody's on my side. You just want to know if I'm lying," he replied bitterly. "Well, my mother's on my side, I guess."

"What about your father?" She raised both of her eyebrows.

"I suppose he is." He shook his head. "He's my father, so yeah, I guess he's on my side. It's hard to tell." He thought for a moment. "I don't remember seeing him at the hospital, but they—Mom—said he came a lot when I wasn't conscious. Just seems weird to me that I was asleep every time he came to see me."

"And what about your brother? Isn't he on your side, too?"

He didn't answer. He closed his eyes and heard Danny's voice shouting, *You killed Sean. You're just faking amnesia so you can get away with it.*

He hadn't believed Danny's apology. Mom had made him do it, and it was obvious he hadn't meant a word of it.

"Eric, whatever you tell me is in confidence. I can't tell anyone anything you tell me," she reminded him gently. "All I am bound to tell the police is whether or not I believe you have amnesia, and my assessment of your mental state based on our talk. I'm not trying to trap you." She smiled—but the smile didn't quite reach her eyes. "That's not my job."

He folded his arms and shrugged. "So you say. But you do work for the police, don't you?"

"You feel hostility toward me?" Her voice stayed even and calm.

"I don't feel anything for you," he said with a slight shrug of his shoulders. "I just met you. I don't know anything about you."

"So why won't you answer me about your brother?"

Ah, what the hell. He gave her a crooked smile. "Okay. Danny—my brother thinks I killed Sean Brody. He also doesn't seem to like me very much. I have no idea why, so don't bother asking. I didn't recognize him the first time I saw him, either. Like everyone else, he was a total stranger to me."

She leaned back in the chair. "Why do you think your brother thinks you're guilty?"

"I don't *know!*" He took a deep breath and gave her another look. "But then I really don't know much of anything anymore." He looked back up at the ceiling. "I told you. I look at my mother and I don't feel anything. I know I'm supposed to love her, but I don't feel *anything* when I look at her. That kind of sucks, you know? Am I some kind of freak? Who doesn't love their mother? The first time I saw her—when I woke up in the hospital—I had no idea who she was. Now I know she's my mother—but I don't feel anything at all. I don't remember her."

"How does that make you feel?" She pursed her lips and scratched her head.

"How does that make me feel?" He stared at her. "How do you think that makes me feel?" He ran his hand over his head. "I don't know who I am, Dr. Guzman. I don't know what kind of a person I was before all of this happened. I don't remember my family. I don't remember my friends. I don't remember a *fucking* thing." He balled his hands into fists. "It's frustrating. Every once in a while"—he hesitated before continuing—"I get this feeling, you know, that something is familiar, like my mind is this close to remembering, and then it's gone."

"What's it like when you try to remember?"

He frowned. "It's like there's this gray fog in my head. I remember things since I woke up—very clearly. But anything from before that time is lost in the fog and no matter how hard I try to remember it's not there." He debated for a moment inside his head, and then shrugged. "Today I remembered a football game I played in. It was like being there again. I saw everything. I could hear the crowd cheering. I was lined up in the backfield waiting for the ball snap. I remember the entire play, up until the time I got knocked out—"

"You were knocked out? How?"

He shrugged. "I don't know. I got hit from both sides, I remember that much, and I fell into the end zone as I was blacking out. When I came to, I was being helped to the sidelines and we won the game. I remember all of it. I remember the game ending, and my girlfriend running out onto the field. And then the fog came back. And I couldn't remember anything else."

"How did that make you feel?" She leaned forward again, her face an expressionless mask.

"It was frustrating." Eric nodded. "It makes me want to punch something. But I don't. I don't punch anything. Dr. Weston taught me some relaxation exercises before I left the hospital, so when I get frustrated, I do that. It always helps."

"You don't see that as a positive thing?" Her voice was curious. "You don't see getting flashes of memory as a good thing for you?"

"I guess it's a good thing. But it's hard to get excited about remembering a stupid dinner or a football game when what everyone wants me to remember is if I killed Sean Brody or not." He rubbed his eyes. "That's what *I* want to remember."

"But you do remember him being shot now, and you weren't the one who shot him. Doesn't that ease your mind?"

"Some, I guess." He shrugged. "But I don't know who did shoot him, Dr. Guzman. And I don't know if anyone's going to believe I'm not making this whole thing up unless I remember who did do it." He thought about it for a moment and decided to tell her. "I signed onto my Facebook page this morning, and there was a message from Sean that morning, wanting me to meet him at the Ledge." He leaned back against the wall and closed his eyes. "So, *he* was the one who wanted to meet me out there. I didn't lure him out there."

"Were the two of you friends?"

"No, we weren't even friends on Facebook." He opened his eyes and gave her a wry smile. "We were when we were kids. But we weren't anymore. I don't remember why." He swallowed. "My friend Chris—" He broke off.

"Yes? What about Chris?" she probed.

"Chris says it was because Sean was gay."

"You sound like you don't believe that."

Eric shook his head. "It just doesn't seem *right*, Dr. Guzman. It seems like a stupid reason to stop being friends."

"It seems stupid to you?" Dr. Guzman leaned back in her chair. "A lot of people think that's a really great reason to not like someone, to hate people." She sighed. "Just a few weeks ago a gay teenager hanged himself over in Oakhurst because he was being bullied."

He felt nauseous. "That's *terrible*."

But—it seemed *familiar.*

He closed his eyes and leaned back against the wall. *Come on, come on*, he urged himself. *Why does that sound familiar?*

"Eric, are you all right?"

It was gone.

He opened his eyes and looked at her. "Yes. That story—I don't know, it seemed familiar. I was trying to remember."

"It happened about a week before your accident." She shrugged. "It was pretty big news, I'm sure you heard about it. Sadly, it happens rather frequently."

"It's wrong," he replied vehemently.

"So, if Sean was gay, you don't think you would have killed him for that?"

"I didn't kill him. I told you." He bit his bottom lip. "I don't know. I can't possibly know. I told you I don't know who I am— who I was." In spite of himself he felt tears rising in his eyes. "I don't want to think I could kill someone. I don't want to believe I could. But what choice do I have?"

"You always have a choice, Eric."

"Yeah." She seemed nice and sympathetic, like she truly was on his side in all of this. But he still wasn't completely sure he could trust her. "There's something else, too." He swallowed. "Maybe I was like this before, I don't know, but when I touch people—"

"Yes?"

"You'll think I'm crazy."

She didn't answer him, just watched him until the silence became uncomfortable. Finally she said, "What happens when you touch people, Eric?"

"Sometimes when I touch someone I can see into their minds," he whispered, watching her face.

She didn't change expression. After a moment, she smiled and held out her right hand. "Show me."

He took her hand—

—I've never heard of anything like this before. I wonder if this is a symptom of the concussion? I've never heard of someone with amnesia having this. I'll have to consult with Dr. Freneau at UCLA—

He pulled his hand away. "Do you think Dr. Freneau could help?"

She was staring at her hand. She looked up at him. She opened her mouth but no sound came out. She cleared her throat. "When—when did you first experience this—this side effect?"

He closed his eyes and rested his head against the pillow. "It's happened a couple of times. Once, when I was in the hospital, I dreamed one of my nurses had fallen asleep with a cigarette in her hand and set her apartment on fire. I rang for the nurse and made her call to make sure Latrice was okay. The fire department was there." He thought for a moment. "That's the only time something like *that* has ever happened. But when I touch people—hand to hand—I can hear what they're thinking. Like just now, with you. You were thinking you'd never heard of anything like this before, you were wondering if it was a symptom of the concussion, you wanted to consult with Dr. Freneau at UCLA."

"Interesting." She leaned forward in her chair. Her eyes narrowed as she stared at him. "You read my mind. That's exactly what I was thinking." A corner of her mouth lifted. A dimple formed in her right cheek. She scribbled some notes onto her pad. She looked back up at him, and held her right hand out again. "Do it again."

He thought about refusing—there was something about this he didn't like—but he took her hand again.

This has to be bullshit. There's no such thing as ESP or telepathy. That's junk science. It was uncanny that he knew who

*Dr. Freneau was and that I was thinking about him, but it doesn't
mean anything. It could have just been coincidence—*

"Of course it could have been coincidence," he said as he
let go of her hand. "And maybe it is all just junk science, I don't
know, but can you come up with an explanation?"

This time the color drained out of her face.

He smiled at her. "You want to try again?"

"No, I don't think so." She rubbed her hand where he'd
touched her. "It's very curious. I feel—I felt—I felt like you—you
were in my head. I knew you were there. Fascinating." Her face
lit up with curiosity. "You know, I read a study—" She paused.
"There's a lot we don't know about the brain, Eric, and what it
can do." She shook her head. "I'm definitely going to put in a call
to Dr. Freneau. I won't tell him anything other than—other than
this strange ability you seem to have. Would you mind talking to
him, if he's interested in your case?"

"Sure," Eric replied. "It can't hurt, I guess."

She pushed her chair back. "He'll want to run some tests on
you." She glanced at her watch. "Oh, dear, we're about out of
time. I'd like to talk to you again sometime, if you don't mind—
not on police business." Her eyes shone. "And you're sure you
don't mind talking to Dr. Freneau?"

"If you think it's a good idea." He watched as she got out
of the chair. Her hand was shaking as she reached for her purse.
She's afraid of me, he realized. *I've scared the crap out of her.*

She paused at the door and took a deep breath. She turned and
looked back at him. "Thank you, Eric. It was"—she swallowed—
"very enlightening talking to you."

The door closed behind her.

Eric lay back on the bed and stared at the ceiling. *What
now?*

CHAPTER EIGHT

Lacey showed up after lunch.

Lunch had been quietly excruciating. Danny was off at baseball practice, so it was just Eric and his mother. She looked terrible, and he felt guilty. The stress and strain of everything was showing on her face—which was pale with deep dark circles under her eyes. She gave him a weak smile when she placed a plate with two Sloppy Joe's on sesame seed buns in front of him. As he ate, he couldn't help but notice she wasn't eating. She wouldn't look at him, either. She kept her eyes on her plate as she fidgeted with her sandwich—which she eventually tossed into the trash half-eaten.

"Mom," he finally said when he couldn't take the silence any longer, "I'm sorry about all this."

Her bloodshot eyes got watery, and she just patted his hand. "It's not your fault, son," she replied, her voice quivering.

He didn't have much of an appetite himself, but he forced himself to eat every bit of the food on his plate. When he was finished, she took his plate without a word and started washing dishes in the sink. He pushed his chair away from the table and stood. He wondered whether he should say something—but what could he say to make her feel better?

Feeling like an utter failure as a son, he went out to the front porch.

When Lacey drove up in her red Honda, he was sitting on the porch swing, reviewing the session with Dr. Guzman in his head, wondering if he shouldn't have told her about the weird mind-reading thing. But she had believed him—he'd seen it in her eyes, and it had freaked her out just a little, despite how outwardly calm she had remained.

He couldn't blame her. How was it possible that he could read people's minds just by touching their hands?

It didn't make sense. *I wouldn't think it was possible either if it weren't happening to me*, he reminded himself. *But maybe this Dr. Freneau can help with it—and maybe he can help me get my memory back.*

Lacey smiled as she got out of her car and walked across the lawn. She was wearing jean shorts that hugged her and an untucked baggy white T-shirt. "Hey," she said, climbing up onto the porch. She fidgeted with her keys for a moment before dropping them into her shoulder bag. "How are you feeling?" she asked, hesitating for just a moment before sitting down on the swing next to him.

"Okay," he replied, smiling back at her. "Not much pain anymore—just when I do something stupid and my ribs will let me know they don't approve." He laughed. "But I'm not taking any more pain pills. I'm tired of feeling loopy and out of it."

She briefly touched his leg with her left hand. "That's good, Eric." She looked away almost immediately.

"Something wrong?" he asked. *She's afraid to touch me, afraid I'll read her mind again.*

The thought filled him with sadness.

"It's just—" She wiped at her eyes. "I'm sorry. It's just, you know, whenever I used to pick you up you always were waiting for me here, in the swing." She gave him a slight shrug. "When I pulled up and saw you sitting here—well, it reminded me of—" She shook her head. "Never mind."

"The way things used to be?" he answered, wanting to take her hand but afraid to at the same time.

She nodded. "Yeah. I wish we could go back to the way things used to be," she said in a low voice.

"Yeah," he replied, looking away from her and at a big blue truck driving by. It looked kind of like Chris's, and it was driving slow. But once it went past their driveway, it sped up. "I know this whole situation sucks, and I'm sorry about that. I wish I could make it easier for you. For everyone."

"That's so sweet—but it's not nearly as hard on me or anyone else as it is on you. The last thing you need to be worrying about is my feelings. I don't deserve that—you need to focus on you. Me? I'll be fine, okay?"

"This is killing my mother," Eric replied. "And Danny."

"Danny." She rolled her eyes.

"He really hates me." Eric looked down at his hands. "He accused me the other night of faking the amnesia and killing Sean. He really thinks I did it, Lacey. My own brother."

"Don't let Danny upset you." She put her hand down on his leg.

Without a thought, he put his down on top of hers.

Danny is jealous of you. It's not easy being the younger brother of the football star. He doesn't think he can measure up. He thinks everyone judges him as a failure because he isn't you. It's also not your fault. What are you supposed to do? Throw a game to make him feel better? But deep down, he's a good kid. He worships you and is jealous at the same time.

She pulled her hand away, rubbing it like it was burned.

"I'm sorry," he whispered. "I shouldn't have done that."

She looked at him, her eyes wide. "Eric, what's that all about?" She kept her voice low. "It happened in the hospital—whenever you—you *touch* me, I—I don't know, it's like…it's like you're in my mind." She shook her head and laughed. "That sounds crazy, doesn't it? Maybe I should stop watching scary movies."

"I don't know how it happens," he whispered. "I don't know what causes it."

She bit her lower lip. "So, when I visited you in the hospital, and you knew about me and Chris—it wasn't because you remembered—it was because *you read my mind*?" She stared at him, her eyes round. "That isn't possible! It's like something from a movie. Or from *Supernatural.*"

"I don't know how or why it happens." He couldn't meet her eyes. "I just woke up this way in the hospital, and I don't know if it happens every time, or with everybody. I'm kind of afraid to find out."

"What does your doctor think?"

"He doesn't know. I—I haven't told him."

She didn't answer for a moment. "Maybe you should. Maybe it has something to do with your memory being gone."

"I told the police psychiatrist. She came to see me this morning." He laughed. "I did it to her—twice."

"Wow." She grinned. "Did it freak her out?"

"A little—but she was more interested than anything else. She's going to talk to some other doctor with more experience with this kind of thing." He leaned back in the swing, which started moving back and forth a bit. "I kind of feel like a freak."

She narrowed her eyes. "Maybe it'll stop when your memory comes back."

"Maybe." He shrugged. "I wish it would stop now. I don't like it, Lacey. It creeps me out."

"Well, you're not a freak." She touched the side of his face. "Don't ever think that."

"I don't know what I am," he replied bitterly. "I don't know who I was, I don't know who I am."

"Your memory will come back, I believe that."

"It's starting to, I think." Hesitantly, he started telling her about the memory flashes he'd been having. Once he started talking, though, the words started pouring out of him. It felt good to unburden himself to someone—someone who wasn't judging him, or evaluating him for the police.

He stopped himself when he got to the part about the gunshot in the woods. Instead, he simply told her he heard a shot and remembered being back on the Ledge with Sean.

"But, Eric, that's great." She started to put her hand on his arm, but stopped herself. Quickly she went on, "You know you didn't kill Sean! That must be a big relief to you!"

"But I don't know why he wanted me to meet him out there." He swallowed. "When I went on Facebook this morning, there was a message from him that morning, wanting me to meet him at the Ledge. He said he couldn't go on the way things were and wanted me to meet him. I can't remember why. And if we weren't friends anymore—why would I go out there? It doesn't make any sense. That's why I asked you to come over, Lacey. I need your help."

"Of course. Anything I can do, just ask." She smiled. "I'd be glad to help you any way I can, Eric. That hasn't changed."

"I need to talk to Bob Nowicki and Kerry Gargaro," he replied.

"Bob and Kerry? Why?"

"They're Sean's friends, and they might be able to help me figure out what was going on that day."

"Yes, they were Sean's friends, and help you do what?" She

tilted her head to one side. "You remembered they were Sean's friends?" A delighted smile started spreading across her face. "But, but that's really great!"

He smiled back at her. "Don't get too excited. I didn't remember—I looked through the yearbook and saw a picture of them, and figured it out from there. They might be able to—" he broke off. "Lacey, how well did you know Sean?"

"Well, I've known him—knew him, I mean, since we were kids." She shrugged. "We weren't friends, but I liked him, thought he was nice."

"Did you know he was gay?" he asked, watching closely for her reaction.

"Wow." She blew out her breath. "No, I didn't know that." She tilted her head to one side again. "But how do you know that?"

He explained everything to her carefully—from the conversation with Chris, to the memory triggered in the woods by the gunshot. He also told her about the message exchange with Bob on Facebook. "So, what I'm hoping is, one, you'll take me out to the Ledge, and two, you'll get me together with Kerry and Bob."

"The Ledge," she breathed. "I haven't been out there since—" She looked away.

"Since the party when you slept with Chris?"

Her spine stiffened, and she looked him directly in the eyes. "Yes. Not since then."

"Maybe when I get my memory back I'll be upset about that," he said slowly, "but you know what? Right now, I don't care."

"It's weird," she replied, "but—"

"But what?"

"I think I like you better now than I did before."

He laughed. "You up for going out there right now?"

She nodded.

He didn't tell his mother where they were going—just that he was going for a ride with Lacey. She was obviously so happy he was doing anything with Lacey, he mused, that he could have told her they were going out to the Ledge and she wouldn't have objected. "Just be back in time for dinner," was all she said. "And remember, Danny's game is tonight."

Just like when he came home from the hospital, nothing on the drive through town looked the least bit familiar to him—even the high school with its football stadium, where he'd been the big hero on campus. They didn't talk much as the car turned through the streets, with Lacey occasionally waving at someone in another car. Once, when they were stopped at a red light, he noticed the driver of another car staring at him. He didn't recognize the girl, and he didn't say anything to Lacey about her. *Might as well get used to being stared at*, he thought. *It's going to happen a lot when I start leaving the house—unless I can get this whole thing figured out.*

He finally drummed up the nerve to ask her, "Lacey, was I an asshole?"

Startled, she took her eyes off the road for a moment to look over at him, a shocked look on her face. "Why would you say that?"

He took a deep breath. "Lacey, apparently I stopped being friends with Sean because I thought he was gay. That sounds like an asshole to me."

She stopped at another light. "Look, you weren't perfect by any means—no one is. You had your moments. Sometimes you did and said things I didn't like." She tapped her fingers on the steering wheel. "I wasn't honest before."

"I need to know."

"You were mean to Sean." she went on. "We used to fight about it all the time. You and some of the other guys—you were just *awful* to him sometimes. You used to say you didn't mean anything by it, it was funny—but *fag* is such an ugly word. It never made sense to me. You didn't hate gay people. I never understood why you singled out Sean, but—" She shook her head. "I guess the campout story kind of explains it. But…"

"But what?"

She sighed. "The morning you left for Santa Barbara, we had a big fight about it. That kid in Oakhurst—Paul Benson—the news had just come out about him hanging himself because kids were picking on him, bullying him for being gay. You were so upset about it, and I couldn't believe it. I told you what you did to Sean was no different than what those kids did to Paul Benson, and you got really mad." The light changed, and she hit the gas pedal. "Then you left town, and that night I got drunk at that party, and…" Her voice trailed off.

He rested his head against the window. "So, maybe there was just a little bit of payback going on?" *I was a bully*, he thought, ashamed.

"Maybe. I don't know." Lacey sighed. "And then a week later—"

"Sean's dead and maybe I killed him."

This is why everyone thinks I killed him. I bullied him, made fun of him, made his life miserable, and then he winds up shot to death and I'm there.

"I never thought that, not once," she replied. "No. Paul Benson's suicide really shook you up, Eric, you were really upset about it. I thought—I thought it was because what happened to him, what those kids were doing to him, was so much like what you and your friend were doing to Sean. That's *why* I never believed for a minute you killed him."

"Okay." Eric closed his eyes. "I was a horrible person, wasn't I?"

"Stop saying that!" she snapped. "Or I'm taking you back home right now!"

"Sorry," he replied, not meaning it. He looked out the window and didn't say another word.

In another few minutes they were outside of town and driving through the woods. It was a beautiful day, no clouds in the blue sky overhead and no other cars on the road. Lacey turned the volume on the stereo down. "We're almost to the place where your car went off the road," she said softly. "Do you want to stop?"

He nodded, his pulse quickening.

They were almost at a big curve in the road, and she pulled over on the right shoulder. He got out of the car and stared at the road.

Two black skid marks led from the start of the curve to the shoulder. The guardrail was ripped off halfway through, the jagged metal bent and scarred where his car must have gone through it. He crossed over to the other side. His heart was pounding in his ears as he carefully approached the torn guardrail. He looked over the side.

The incline was incredibly steep, dropping down at around a seventy-degree angle from the road. He could see scars in the vegetation. The incline leveled off beside a clump of pine trees. Pieces of broken glass glittered in the bright sunlight. There was a car-shaped wound in the ground just before the tree line.

That must be where the car landed, he thought, his eyes filling with tears. He wiped at them as Lacey put her arm around his waist, gently rubbing his side with her free hand.

"It was a horrible wreck," she said in a quiet voice. "They had to pry you and Sean both out of the car." Her voice broke as she continued, "I came out before they took the car away—they left it there for a couple of days. It never caught fire—it was a miracle. There were a lot of miracles that day, Eric. When I saw the car"—this time she did sob—"I couldn't believe anyone got out of it alive."

He closed his eyes and felt a chill as a cloud passed over the sun.

Sean didn't get out of the car alive.

He tried to remember.

There was just gray fog.

And a feeling—

"I think I was supposed to die that day," he whispered. "But for some reason, it didn't happen."

"Don't say things like that. Don't ever say something like that, Eric."

But somehow he *knew* he was right.

He wasn't supposed to live.

But somehow, for some reason he didn't understand and couldn't fathom, he had.

"Can we get out of here?" he whispered, unable to take his eyes off the scar in the ground. "I don't like it here."

"Sure. Get back in the car." She gently touched his back.

Another vehicle drove past as she was starting her engine—a blue Ford pickup truck with gigantic tires. The driver blew his horn and she responded by doing the same. "Who is that?" Eric asked as he put his seat belt on.

"Coach Walton." She grinned at him. "Your football coach?"

He shook his head. "I have no idea who he is. His truck looks just like Chris's."

"Yeah." she replied with a grin. "You used to tease him about trying to be like Coach Walton all the time. It drove him nuts."

She put the car into gear and pulled back out onto the road. They drove in silence for another mile or so before she slowed down and turned left onto a dirt road that was barely noticeable. They drove down a sharp incline with trees close on either side.

It was a memory, he thought as he involuntarily pressed the soles of his feet against the floorboards of the car. *I remember this road, I remember these trees, only I was driving the other way.*

After about five minutes they came out into a wide clearing and she parked the car.

The clearing was big enough for maybe about thirty cars to park, and was loose gravel and dirt over hard rock. He got out of the car and stared. It was a ledge, all right—about thirty feet away from where the road came out was the edge. There was no railing or fence. "Isn't that kind of dangerous?" He pointed to the edge.

"It's about a forty-foot drop down to the creek." Lacey shut her car doors. "No one's ever fallen off—no matter how drunk they get. Besides, we usually just leave the cars here and climb down to the creek. There's a trail just over there, to the right—you see, between those two bushes? That's how you climb down. The creek's really the place where everyone hangs out and parties. Everyone just calls the whole place the Ledge."

He looked around in every direction, trying to get his bearings. He closed his eyes and tried to remember where he and Sean had been standing.

I carried him to my car, which was parked about right where Lacey's is. I ran for a good ten, maybe fifteen yards while I carried him, and so—

He paced off fifteen yards, and looked around. It wasn't the right place.

He walked back to the car while Lacey watched, shading her eyes from the bright sun. He marked off another fifteen yards.

"It was right here," he called over to her. He heard her footsteps coming up behind him. He turned around, trying to place the background he remembered. *There*, he thought, when the view was exactly as he remembered. He had his back to the road and to Lacey's car. "I was standing right here, looking at Sean. He was about a yard away from me when I heard the shot, and then he went down." He took a few steps forward. "Right here." He knelt down. He looked back at Lacey. "They know it happened here, don't they?"

She shrugged. "I don't know. I don't think anyone knows where he was shot. All anyone knows is where you wrecked your car and he was in it at the time."

He stared at the dirt and gravel, trying to see if there was anything there—he reached down and picked up a round stone, turning it over in his hands.

The rock had a dark, crusty brown film on the under side.

"Is that—blood?" Lacey's voice caught.

"I think so. This is where it happened." He straightened back up, slipping the rock into his pocket. "Has it rained since the accident?"

"It rained the next day." Lacey scratched her head. "It rained all day and all through the night."

"Probably washed the blood off the top of the rocks." He turned another one over with his shoe. It had the same film on the bottom. "Can you call my uncle on your phone?"

She shook her head. "You can't get cell reception out here, Eric. It's one of the reasons kids come out here to party—their parents can't call them."

He turned and looked behind them. The ledge eventually curved back into the incline of the wooded slope. "I suppose they know if he was shot from the front or from behind," Eric mused.

"If he was shot from the front, the killer had to be in those trees back there." He gestured with his hand. "If he was shot from behind, the killer was back there somewhere." He narrowed his eyes. The ledge didn't curve back into the slope of the mountain at its other end; there it just ended. There were trees beyond where the shelf ended, but there was no way to get into those trees without climbing down from the road or up from the creek bed below.

"He had to be shot from the front," Lacey breathed. "So, you had your back to the killer. You couldn't have seen who it was."

That wasn't very reassuring. Eric turned and looked in the direction where the bullet must have come from. All he saw was pine trees and thicket.

Something else was bothering him. "You said no one knew where it happened, right?"

She nodded.

"Then how did he get here? In my memory, there weren't any other cars out here." Eric scratched his head. "If he didn't drive out here—did he ride with me? Then why did he need to come out here and talk in the first place? He asked me to come out here. I'd think there would be any number of places back in town we could have talked in private without anyone knowing, right?"

Lacey nodded. "Sean didn't have a car. He rode a bike everywhere. He's ridden his bike out here before."

"Well, if he rode his bike out here that day, it's not here now. I suppose someone could have taken it since then if it was abandoned out here." He closed his eyes and replayed the memory. "But I don't remember seeing his bike out here. So, we need to figure out how he got out here."

Lacey grinned. "I guess that's what we do next, right?"

He grinned back at her. "Yeah."

They walked back to her car. As Lacey got in, Eric took one last look around.

Nothing.

He still couldn't remember anything else.

CHAPTER NINE

"So, you think maybe Sean rode out here with his killer?" Lacey asked as she started the car.

"That doesn't make any sense," Eric replied. "I mean, it's not like my memory is all that great, right?" He laughed at himself. "Just because I don't remember seeing his bike doesn't mean it wasn't out here—I just didn't see it in the moments after he was shot and I carried him to the car. But we should find out what happened to his bike. I mean, if it's at his house—that means he got out there that day some other way, right?"

Lacey drove up the inclined dirt road. "You want me to check with his mother?"

"Well, I don't think she'd be willing to talk to me, do you?" Eric sighed.

"Most likely not," Lacey replied. "I mean, I hate to tell you this—"

"I'd rather know than not," Eric replied, irritated. "I'm tired of being treated like a baby by everyone. I have amnesia. It didn't turn me into a baby, for Christ's sake."

Lacey started laughing.

"What's so funny?" he demanded.

She wiped at her eyes. "That sounded like the old Eric."

She grinned at him. "Boy, did you hate being treated like a kid! Nothing made you madder." She blew out her breath. "Okay, then. Mrs. Brody is leading the 'Eric Matthews is a murderer' brigade in town."

"Why wouldn't she?" he replied, puzzled. "She thinks I killed her son."

Lacey glanced at him. "Okay."

Instead of turning right when the car reached the paved county road, Lacey turned to the left.

"Where are you going?" Eric asked, confused. "Isn't town the other way?"

"I need gas, and there's a Shell station about a half-mile this way." She grinned at him and winked. "You used to get mad at me all the time because I always would forget to put gas in my car—that hasn't changed. I just never think to pay attention to the gauge! I remember this one time we were driving down to the mall in Merced and I forgot to get gas and we ran out, and you were so furious with me...you had to walk almost a mile in the rain to get help and I..."

He stopped listening to her story of what really was a *you weren't always the best boyfriend* story and looked out the window at the trees passing by on the side of the road. The rock in his pocket felt hot. It was important, he knew—the police could test the blood on the rock and determine if it was Sean's or not. Maybe it wouldn't clear him of the murder, but it was a step in the right direction. If the police knew where the shooting actually took place, maybe there was some other evidence they could find that *would* clear him.

And there was the question of Sean's bike. How had he gotten out to the Ledge? There was no sign of his bike there. Maybe the killer had taken it—but why? If Sean hadn't ridden his bike to the Ledge, then someone must have given him a lift—but it seemed a little strange the person hadn't come forward—

Unless Sean's killer gave him the ride out there.

But why? Why would Sean have ridden out there with someone who wants to kill him, to meet me? he wondered. *It doesn't make any sense. But if Sean didn't know—*

He leaned his head against the window and closed his eyes.

"You haven't been listening to a word I'm saying, have you?" Lacey lightly slapped his knee. "Even with amnesia, some things never change."

"I'm sorry." He opened his eyes and smiled back at her. "My mind just drifted for a little bit."

"Nothing out there helped you remember anything, did it?" Lacey sighed. "I'm sorry, too, Eric. I kind of hoped—"

"So did I," he admitted. "I guess I'm not going to be able to force my memory back—it'll come back when it wants to." *If it ever does*, he added to himself. "Did we go out there a lot? I have lots of pictures of us out there. What else can you tell me about the Ledge?"

"Well, we didn't go there a lot." She frowned. "I mean, it's a popular place for kids to go, but most kids go out there to drink and get high—but we didn't do either." She shrugged. "You were always really focused on being in shape for sports, and you didn't drink or smoke, which was fine with me. I don't really, either. Every once in a while—" She flushed.

"You're not used to drinking." He smiled at her. "I'm sure that had something to do with you and Chris—well, you know." *She was drinking, and we'd had a fight before I left town*, he thought. *But what was Chris's reason for doing it?*

Lacey was mad at me, got drunk, and "punished" me by sleeping with Chris. But why did Chris do it? He said he was drunk—but was that enough of a reason to make a play for his best friend's girlfriend? I think I need to talk to him again, I don't think he was being completely honest with me. And if worst comes to worst, I can always touch him and read his mind.

"We would go out there to lay out and get tan, swim in the creek, but it wasn't a place we usually just went by ourselves to hang out, you know—we always went out there with groups, for parties and things. We never went out there alone." She tapped her fingers on the steering wheel.

"But kids come out here all the time?"

"I don't really know." She shrugged. "I guess. I know some of the stoner kids come out here to hang out in the woods and get stoned and stupid, but—why do you ask?"

"I was just wondering why no one was out there the day Sean was shot." He rubbed his eyes. "I mean, if it was a hangout, how come we were there alone? It doesn't make sense. If he wanted to talk to me privately, why go to a place where there wasn't a guarantee we'd be alone? Why would he want to meet me there, of all places? I mean, you said he rode his bike everywhere—but isn't that a little far for him to go?"

"He'd ridden out there before," Lacey replied. "I don't know why there wasn't anyone else there that day." She frowned, wrinkling her forehead. After a moment, she smacked herself in the head. "Sorry, I'm really stupid sometimes! The fair!"

"The fair?"

She laughed. "The county fair, Eric. It opened that day. That's where everyone was. I didn't go—but it was a pretty safe bet no one would be out there."

"Okay, then where is his bike?"

"Well, the killer could have taken it, or someone else could have come along later and stolen it," she replied matter-of-factly.

"I mean, if it was just sitting there, anyone could have taken it—it's been three weeks since Sean was shot."

That hadn't occurred to him. "But there had to be better places for him to meet me. Why did he want me to meet him all the way out here?" He slammed his fist down on the console between them. "I wish I could remember!"

"Calm down, Eric." She slowed down as the car went around a curve. A Shell sign appeared just ahead on the left through the trees. "Maybe it's important—maybe it's not. There could have been any number of reasons why Sean wanted you to come out here—but the only person who we know knew for sure was Sean himself, and he's not able to tell us anything."

"Yeah." He took a few deep breaths and felt himself calming down. "I do think the bike is important, though."

"I'll go ahead and check with Mrs. Brody." She flashed a grin as she turned into the lot and pulled up to an outside island. "I can say I'm looking for a birthday present for my brother Denny." She turned the car off and pulled her wallet out of her purse. She fished out a five and handed it to him. "Will you go inside and get me a Diet Coke? I'm parched. Get yourself something if you're thirsty." She opened her car door. "It'll be okay, Eric. You *will* remember."

Easy for you to say, he thought bitterly as he got out of the car and stretched. There was a twinge from his ribs, but it wasn't so bad—nothing he couldn't handle. He walked across to the little store. There was a big white cooler with metal doors to the left of the entrance with *Ice* written in large pale blue letters across the top. The windows were filled with signs advertising sales and the availability of lottery tickets. The lot was paved, but the pavement turned into gravel just beyond the corners of the store, and there was another big drop-off down the slope of the mountain a few yards beyond where the gravel ended with a big steel guardrail. He opened the door, and cold air enveloped him as he stepped inside to the chime of a bell. There were three rows of various things—the closest one was stocked with plastic containers of various kinds of motor oil and other car maintenance things. There was a station for filling out lottery tickets to his left, and beyond that a magazine stand. The wall to his far left was coolers, as was the entire wall directly opposite the front door. He started walking to the coolers to his left, since *Coke* was written in white script on a red background across their tops. Out of the corner of his eye he noticed the girl working behind the counter staring at him, her mouth open in a circle. She was holding a small bag of Doritos in her left hand.

Great, he thought, opening the cooler and grabbing two bottles of Diet Coke, *just what I need*. He grimaced and walked up the center aisle, bags of chips on one side and candy on the other. He placed the bottles on the counter and smiled at the girl.

Her mouth was now closed, but she was still staring at him, the Doritos bag still in her hand. She was wearing brown polyester slacks with a slight tear along the outer seam on her left leg. She was wearing worn-out sandals, and a polyester smock in an ugly shade of pale blue. There were two pink barrettes holding back her lusterless brown hair. Her face was round with narrow lips, a crooked nose, and a cluster of pimples in various stages of development across her forehead. Her eyes were her best feature—large, round, and a rich, deep brown.

"Hello, Eric," she said. Her voice was soft. She picked up a handheld scanner and ran it over the scanner symbols. The cash register beeped twice. There was a name tag on her blazer, with *Karly* underneath the Shell logo. "I'm really glad you're out of the hospital."

Startled, he didn't answer at first—not knowing what to say. He'd been expecting—*I don't know what I was expecting, but not kindness.* "Thanks," he finally managed to mutter. He looked down at the counter, sticking his hands into his shorts pockets and shifting his weight from one foot to the other.

"Not everyone believes you killed Sean, you know," she went on. "I never believed it for a minute. You're not a killer."

He felt his eyes fill with tears, so he kept looking down. "Thanks. I really appreciate that."

"People can be quite mean-spirited, can't they?" she went on in her soft, soothing voice. "But there are a lot more people rooting for you than against you. We may not have been friends"—she laughed—"you probably didn't even know I existed, but I could tell you weren't like the others."

"Others?" He looked into those soft brown eyes. "What do you mean?"

"Chris Moore, Tessa Doyle." She waved a hand dismissively. "They're your friends, all right, but that doesn't mean you're like them. Someone tells me Chris Moore shot somebody, that I'd believe. But not you." She shook her head. "You're kind, Eric. A lot of people look at you and might see a good-looking boy who's full of himself and shallow—but there's more to you than that. You're a sleeping angel."

"A what?" He couldn't have heard that right. "What did you say?"

"I said you were a sleeping angel." She laughed again. "The potential to do great good is inside you—you just don't know it yet."

He tried to answer, but couldn't find the words.

"That'll be two fifty-three." She smiled when he looked up. "The Diet Cokes?" Her voice was gentle.

"Oh, yeah, of course." He dug Lacey's five out of his pocket and handed it over. She made change, and when she gave it to him their hands touched—

—God has surely placed his mark on Eric. I always knew He would—Eric has always been a good boy if slightly distracted by all the high school foolishness. Look at him! He is practically glowing with God's light. He doesn't seem to know it yet. God hasn't shared his purpose with him yet. Please stay strong, Eric. God needs you to be strong.

He pulled his hand away and the coins scattered across the counter. He stared at her. She just smiled.

It was like she was talking to me—she knew I could hear her thoughts and so she spoke directly to me.

"Are you okay?" Her voice was concerned, but her smile didn't waver. "You look a little pale."

"You—you didn't notice anything, well," he swallowed, "*strange* just now?"

Her smile didn't falter. "Life is full of strange things, Eric. The world—this wonderful, beautiful world God created, is all strange and wonderful, if you just pay attention and take a good look at it all." Her hand went to her neck, and she pulled out a gold chain with a gold cross suspended from it. "You shouldn't fear the unknown—you should embrace the wonder of it all. God always has a plan, you know."

Unnerved, he grabbed the Diet Cokes and walked out of the store without saying good-bye. He could hear his heart pounding in his ears. Lacey was putting the pump back as he walked up to the car. His hand slightly shaking, he held out one of the drinks.

"Thanks." She smiled as she took it from him, but then narrowed her eyes a little bit. "Are you okay? You—you look like you've seen a ghost or something."

He shook his head, trying to calm himself. "That girl inside—"

"Oh, I'm sorry, I should have warned you. I forgot you have amnesia! Isn't that funny? *I forgot.*" She reached up and briefly touched his cheek with her right hand. "What did she say to you? If she said something bad, I swear I'll go in there and smack the snot out of her."

"No." He shook his head. "She was actually really nice. She told me she was glad I'm out of the hospital and she doesn't believe I killed Sean."

"That's Christian Karly. She's really a sweet girl, but she's a little—" She twirled her index finger near her left temple. "Her dad was a preacher, and he was killed in a fire a few years ago. I don't think she's ever gotten over it. She's really into the whole church thing. She thinks God talks to her."

"Seriously?"

"I don't know if it's true or not—she's never actually said that to *me*." She shook her head. "I probably shouldn't repeat things like that. It's just mean gossip, really. She's never said that to me, anyway, but Tessa Doyle—" She sighed. "Then again, Tessa Doyle is a mean bitch and I shouldn't listen to anything she says. What else did Karly say to you?"

Keep your mouth shut, she'll never understand, she'll think you're crazy—even though she's experienced it, he thought. "She just said she was glad I'm out of the hospital."

"See what I mean? That's just sweet." She opened her car door. "Where do you want to go now?"

He opened his mouth to reply when the big blue pickup truck that had passed them earlier slowed down and pulled into the station. It pulled up alongside the far side of Lacey's car, and the passenger window rolled down.

"I thought that was you two I saw earlier," a man said with a Southern accent. Eric couldn't really see him inside the truck. He squinted, but the shadows inside the truck from the darkened windows created too much gloom. "Hey Eric, Lacey. How you two doing?"

The voice, though, sounded familiar,

I know that voice, he thought, and his stomach lurched.

The truck's engine shut off, and the driver's side door opened.

Eric felt goose bumps rising on his arms despite the warmth of the sun, and the hairs on the back of his neck stood up as the man climbed down. He felt panic rising, his stomach lurching, and he desperately wanted to be somewhere, anywhere, else. *Who is this?* he wondered. *And why—*

"Hi there, Coach Walton," Lacey said sweetly, giving Eric a glance to let him know she spoke his name for Eric's benefit. "What are you doing all the way out here?"

"I could ask you two the same question," said the man as he came around the front of the truck, and Eric resisted the urge to run for the store.

Coach Walton was in his early thirties, with thick jet-black hair he wore cropped close to his scalp. He was wearing a white muscle tank top with curly dark hairs sticking out from the neckline. His biceps and shoulders were thickly muscled from hours in the gym. His stomach was flat and his waist narrow. He was wearing khaki shorts, and his legs were hairy and powerful. His forehead was low and thick, his nose jutting out from under it. He wasn't shaven—his cheeks, neck, and chin were covered with blue-black stubble. He was smiling, but it didn't quite reach his narrow eyes. "Me? I was checking out some of the mountain trails," he said pleasantly, stopping and leaning against the side of Lacey's car. He didn't take his eyes off Eric. "Trying to find a

place for the team to run for morning two-a-days next month—
nothing like running up the side of the mountain for conditioning.
How you feeling, Eric? The team needs you this year if we're
going to make a run for the state championship."

Eric opened his mouth, but no words came out. He just stood
there, his stomach churning, resisting the urge to get as far away
from this man as possible.

"Eric just wanted to get out of town," Lacey replied, her
voice still sickeningly sweet. Eric glanced at her out of the corner
of his eyes. "So I thought it would do him some good to get some
fresh air out in the country."

"Fresh air never hurt anyone. You're looking pretty good,"
Coach Walton went on, looking him up and down. "You've
dropped some weight, though. You'll need to put that weight
back on. Make sure you're eating, son. You won't heal if you're
not eating." Coach Walton winked at him. "I'll give your mom
a call, see if we can get you on some protein shakes. Maybe get
you back into the weight room."

"Uh-huh," Eric muttered.

"Think you'll be healthy enough when practice starts next
month? You need me to talk to your doctor?" His grin got wider,
baring his teeth. "Be happy to help out any way I can, son. You're
an important part of the team."

"I don't know," he finally managed to get out. "I—"

"Hurt your ribs, didn't you? And your ankle?"

Eric nodded. "My ankle's a lot better." He closed his eyes,
wishing Coach Walton would just get in his truck and drive away.
"Ribs, too."

"So, I guess it's just your head?" Coach Walton leaned
forward. "You ask me, I would have thought your head was too
hard to get hurt. That's the one place I figured was safe from
injury on you, son." He laughed.

It was an unpleasant sound.

Touch him, see what he's thinking, see if you can find out why you're getting such a bad feeling from him, a voice whispered inside Eric's head. He swallowed. He didn't want to touch Coach Walton. He didn't want to know what was in his head.

"Well, it's good to see you, son, don't hesitate to call if you need anything. You know I'm just up the street from you. You can always just come on over—you're welcome any time. All my boys are," Coach Walton said. "Good seeing you, too, Lacey. Take good care of our star player." He got back into his truck and shut the door. The engine revved for a moment, and the horn honked as it moved off onto the road.

Lacey shivered. "I don't like that man," she said in a low voice. "I never have. I don't like the way he looks at me. It gives me the creeps."

Eric didn't say anything until the blue truck disappeared around the curve. He stood there watching as the goose bumps went down and the sun felt warm on his arms again. He turned back to Lacey. "Let's head back to town." He walked around the car and opened the passenger door.

"What's wrong with you girls?" Coach Walton screamed, spittle flying out of his mouth. "Forgotten how to play football? You want to maybe put on skirts and be cheerleaders? Because you sure as hell aren't playing like men out there!"

Eric looked around the locker room. Everyone had their heads down, the uniforms covered in mud. He took a drink out of a water bottle. The locker room smelled of sweat and disinfectant and mud. His arms were covered in it.

"Nobody's blocking, nobody's tackling, it's like all the time we've spent in practice was a waste of my goddamned time!" Coach Walton went on screaming.

"Eric?"

He shook his head to clear it. "Did we play a muddy game last season?"

"You had another memory?" Lacey's eyes opened wide. "Yes, when we played Central Catholic. It rained all day, and after the game started the field turned into soup. Mud soup. And it started raining again."

His hands were shaking. He grabbed hold of the car with his free hand. He took a gulp of his Diet Coke. His stomach was bothering him, and he sighed. "Well, yeah, I did remember being in the locker room—halftime, I guess, and Coach Walton was chewing us out."

"It wasn't a good game, the conditions were terrible," Lacey said. "I was soaked—I caught a really bad cold and had to spend the weekend in bed." She shuddered. "I remember you were really upset after the game, but you wouldn't say why."

"It probably doesn't matter." He looked at her and gave her a weak smile. "I can't control what memories come back—but it's frustrating when the ones that do are useless."

"Yeah." She winked. "Come on, let's get going."

As he was getting in, he saw Karly standing in the store doorway, holding her gold cross in her hands. She raised her hand in a wave, and then went back inside.

Chapter Ten

Even though he was gone, Eric couldn't shake the feeling he'd gotten from Coach Walton. He shivered again and rolled down his car window. *There was something—something about his eyes*, he thought with a shiver, trying to put his finger on what it was that bothered him.

"Do you want me to turn the air off?" Lacey asked as she waited for an SUV to pass by. "Are you sure you're okay? You look pale."

"I'm fine." He didn't know how to even begin explaining the strange feeling to her, so he decided it was best not to even try. "So that's Coach Walton," he said, trying to keep his voice light. "And I don't remember anything about him. You said you don't like him?"

"He's okay." She pulled out onto the road. "I mean, he's a good coach—we used to *suck* before he came here. We haven't had a losing season since."

"Didn't you say you didn't like the way he looks at you? That he gives you the creeps?"

"Yeah." She started accelerating. "I don't know what it is. Nobody else seems to feel that way about him—but he wins. People wouldn't care if he sacrificed babies to the devil as long as we went to the playoffs every year, you know." She tapped her fingers on the steering wheel. "The way he looks at me—I don't know, it's like he's imagining me out of my clothes. I mean, all guys do that sometimes, but with him, it's like every time." She shuddered. "I don't like it."

"He talks funny." Eric inwardly shivered. *Take good care of our star player.*

He couldn't help feeling there was something ominous in those words.

She made a face. "He's from Mississippi or some place like that," she said, after thinking for a moment. "I'm pretty sure it's Mississippi. He went to Fresno State and played football there, was an assistant coach or something, then got the job up here about three years ago. His wife is nice—they have a little girl about two years old. She's the cutest thing—her name is Willow. Anyway, Mrs. Walton is always pretty friendly. She looks tired all the time—guess that's normal when you have a two-year-old. She always says hello and tallks to us—the cheerleaders—at the games. He's also the P.E. teacher. He's a real hardass." Her mouth twisted. "He's terrible to the kids who aren't athletic, always making fun of them and yelling at them. He's a bully. And he's, I don't know, arrogant? Smug? I can't think of the word. But there's something about him I don't like. He's always friendly, I guess, but it seems kind of fake to me."

"Did I like him? What did I think?"

"I really don't know. You never really said anything one way or the other," Lacey replied. "You never really talked much about football with me—which I appreciated. Some of the guys on the team *never* shut up about it."

"I never said *anything* about him?" Eric scratched his head.

"I know you thought he was a good coach," she replied, raising her left eyebrow. They were driving past the accident site.

Eric bit his lower lip and closed his eyes as the smashed guardrail came into view. "But Chris absolutely *hates* him. He never has anything good to say about Coach Walton."

"Do you know why?" Eric looked at her. *This is important,* he thought, *I need to talk to Chris.*

"You'd have to ask him. He threatens to quit the team all the time, and you always talk him out of it." Lacey's face lit up as she smiled. "My guess is Coach Walton is hard on him. Chris likes things to be easy—he doesn't like having to work. I know he hates having to lift weights and stay in shape in the off-season. Coach Walton is a fanatic about that. You heard him—his main concern about you was how soon you can get back into the weight room—and the weight you've lost." She winked. "I don't know, you look kind of cute all lean and skinny, if you ask me."

She is really pretty, he thought. *I can't believe a girl that pretty would want to be my girlfriend.*

"What?" She glanced over at him. "Why are you looking at me like that? What are you thinking?"

"Oh, nothing—just wondering about Chris." He felt his face coloring, so he turned to look back out the window.

"It must be so hard to not remember anything." She took a deep breath. "Having to ask about your friends and everything—that must be so frustrating for you."

"I don't have much of a choice." He sighed. "Would you mind taking me to the sheriff's office? I think I should probably talk to my uncle, tell him what I've remembered, so they can check out the Ledge." He took another deep breath, feeling the rock in his pocket. "And I have some things I need to ask him."

"Okay. Sure. I can do that." Her voice sounded subdued. After moment, he heard a choked sob.

"Lacey? What's the matter?" he asked, concerned. "Did I say something wrong?"

"I'm sorry." She wiped at her eyes with her left hand. "I'm just, oh, I'm just feeling sorry for myself. I had such—such big plans for this summer and next year." She sighed. "Everything just has—just gone to hell. I can't help but wonder—you know—if I hadn't—you know, with Chris—maybe none of this would happened. I feel *responsible*."

"You're not responsible for what happened, Lacey." Eric turned his head to look out the window again. "Not unless you shot Sean and ran my car off the road somehow."

"I know, but I can't help how I feel." She bit her lip and shook her head. "Okay, enough self-pity! And by the way, I really appreciate you letting me help you with all of this." She smiled at him, and he felt his heart melting a little bit. "I feel like Nancy Drew."

"Who?"

She laughed. "She's a character in books. She solves mysteries."

"Oh, okay. Thanks for helping." He laughed with her. "I'm pretty sure my mom wouldn't have driven me out here. She'd have forbidden me to come out here, I bet. She wants to wrap me in wool or something. She treats me like a baby."

"Can you blame her?" Lacey glanced over at him. "Eric, you almost *died*. You were unconscious for weeks. That had to be rough on her—on your whole family. Danny was really broken up about the whole thing, you know."

"*Danny?*" He made a face. "I don't believe that for a minute."

"You didn't see him." She shook her head. "He was really upset, Eric. He does love you. I mean, I know Danny can be a pain in the ass sometimes, but he really looks up to you."

"Uh-huh." Unconvinced, he closed his eyes and heard

Danny shouting at him again: *You're a killer, and you're just faking amnesia so you can get away with it.*

No, he didn't believe Danny cared about him. Not in the least.

"So, what do you think your uncle's going to say about all this?" Lacey asked. "Are you going to tell him about the mind-reading thing?"

"Well, no, I don't think that's a good idea," Eric said dubiously. "It's too weird. I'm just going to tell him what I've remembered," he tapped the rock in his pocket, "give him this rock, and I have some questions I want to ask him." Eric drummed his fingers against his knee. "For one thing, I want to know what happened to my cell phone—nobody seems to know. And I want to know what happened to the wreck of my car." He leaned his head against the window. "You can just drop me off there. I can call my mom to come pick me up."

"I don't mind at all," she replied brightly. "Really. This is kind of fun—I'm having a good time. I don't have anything else to do." She thought for a moment. "I know—I can hang out in the coffee shop across the street—Mr. Java. While I'm waiting for you, I'll see if I can get Bob and Kerry to meet me there. Hmmm—what can I tell them to get them to come?" She mused for a moment. "I'll think of something." She grinned at him. "Besides, I want to know what your uncle tells you."

"I'm sure you can get them to show up—if anyone can do it, you can." Eric opened his eyes. They were entering the outer reaches of town. Within five minutes she was pulling into a parking space on a block with businesses lined up wall to wall. Across the street was a large stone building with the U.S. and the California state flags moving in the breeze on tall flagpoles. Eric got out of the car and stared at the building. Carved into the stone at the very top were the words *We are a nation of laws not of men.*

"When you're done talking to your uncle, come on over to Mr. Java." Lacey gave him a quick peck on the cheek. "And hopefully, Bob and Kerry will be there. You want me to send you a text if they agree to come?"

"I don't have a phone, remember?"

"Well, you need to get one—talk to your mom about it." She wrinkled her forehead. "What do you think happened to yours?"

He shrugged. "That's what I want to find out." *One thing, at least,* he added to himself. He watched as she walked up the sidewalk and entered the coffee shop before he crossed the street. With every step, his nerves got worse.

He climbed the stairs and walked in through the big double doors. There was a directory mounted on the wall to the left, right next to a desk with a police officer sitting at it. The sheriff's office was on the second floor, so he walked across the polished floor to the big staircase at the back of the lobby. Once he got to the second floor, he could see the door to the sheriff's department at the end of the hall. He got a drink from the water fountain and walked to the door. Just as he reached it, it swung open and he was almost knocked down by someone coming out.

"Oh, excuse me!" the woman said. She had dark black hair teased and sprayed into place, and was wearing too much makeup. She was wearing a tight black T-shirt over a pair of tight black jeans, and a lot of perfume. Her face quickly changed to a scowl. "You." She sneered as she drew her right hand back and slapped him across the face. Startled, he lost his balance and started falling backward. He managed to catch himself by putting his hands on the wall.

His ears ringing and stars dancing in front of his eyes, he still managed to hear her screaming at him.

"Murderer! You're a murderer! You killed my son, you miserable son of a—"

The door to the sheriff's office swung open and two women in uniforms rushed out, grabbed her, and pulled her away from where Eric leaned against the wall. He could feel a headache forming behind his right temple, and his jaw was sore. He closed his eyes as his uncle came rushing out the door. Uncle Arnie asked, "Are you okay?" He knelt down beside Eric, his face concerned.

Eric nodded. He moved his jaw around, and his cheek was still stinging. "I'm getting a headache," he said in a low voice. It was getting worse. "I'm okay, Uncle Arnie."

Uncle Arnie turned to the officers holding the woman and snapped, "Toss her in the holding cell till she cools down. Maybe a little time in the holding cell will do you some good, Gina."

"Oh, that's just perfect!" she spat. "You let a murderer walk the streets—"

"That's enough, Gina." Uncle Arnie's voice tightened, and a vein stood out in his forehead. "He has a concussion! You could have—"

"Killed him?" she threw right back at him. "Good enough for him."

"Ger her out of here." He turned his back on her.

"Yeah, go right ahead! Why don't you just arrest me?" she shouted defiantly. "That would just be perfect! You won't arrest your nephew for killing my son, but you'll arrest ME for giving him the smack he deserves! Oh, that's just perfect, Arnie! You're a disgrace to the uniform!"

His shoulders sagged. "Take her out of here, Clarice, before I do something I regret."

The redheaded lady cop nodded and said, "Now, come along, Mrs. Brody. What were you thinking?"

Mrs. Brody's head dropped and Eric heard a low sob come from her as the officers led her away.

Eric took a deep breath, wincing as his ribs throbbed. "Wow." He gave his uncle a grin. "I sure wasn't expecting that."

"You sure you're okay?" Uncle Arnie asked softly. "Come sit in my office. I'll get you some aspirin. You want me to call the doctor?"

"I'm okay, I don't need the doctor." Eric shook his head. "But I'll take the aspirin. I take it that's Sean's mom?"

Uncle Arnie nodded, opening the door. "Sorry that happened. You picked the wrong time to come down here."

"It's not your fault." Eric walked into the lobby of the office and followed his uncle down another short hallway to another door. His uncle held the door for him. He sat down in a chair on the other side of the desk from his uncle.

"Why are you here?" Uncle Arnie asked. "Does your mother know you're here?"

Eric shook his head. "Lacey brought me. I wanted to talk to you." He hesitated. "I'm starting to remember things. Not much, but here and there."

His face impassive, Arnie nodded. "Okay. Go on."

"Sean was shot out at the Ledge." Eric went on, "Lacey and I went out there before we came here. I remember Sean being shot, Uncle Arnie, and I didn't do it."

"What do you remember?" Arnie leaned forward onto his forearms.

Eric closed his eyes. "We were out there, at the Ledge. Sean was facing me, standing about two yards away from me. He sent me a message on Facebook that morning asking me to meet him there."

"What did the message say?"

"*I can't go on with things the way they are. Can you meet me at the Ledge tomorrow at eleven? We need to talk.*" Eric opened his eyes. "I don't remember why he wanted to talk to me. I don't remember driving out there, or even reading the message—it's still there in my in-box. But I remember us standing there, talking, and then I heard the gunshot from behind me, and Sean's face— he was surprised—and then he went down and there was blood, and I knew I had to get him to the hospital, so I picked him up and carried him to my car." Eric closed his eyes again. "I remember driving out to the county road, but then it just fades away." He reached into his pocket and pulled out the bloodstained rock, placing it on the desk. "I found this out there, right about where he fell after he was shot. I think that's Sean's blood."

Arnie didn't touch the rock. Instead, he leaned back in his chair and put his hands behind his head. "Go on."

Eric looked at him for a moment. "I didn't shoot him, Uncle Arnie."

Arnie's eyes narrowed. "I'll get some people out there to look around."

"Don't you believe me?"

"I want to, son." Arnie blew out a heavy breath. "I don't want to believe my nephew is a killer. But I can't let that affect my investigation—people already think I'm shielding you. I'm getting a lot of pressure from the mayor's office." He rubbed his face with his hands. "It looks bad, son—but I'm also not going to let anyone tell me how to do my job." He blew out a breath. "But it's been weeks, and who knows how many people have been through there? Any evidence we might find will be contaminated. But it's worth a look." He shook his head. "You shouldn't have gone out there, Eric. You should have come to me first."

"Why?" Eric asked, puzzled.

"Because even if we find some evidence out there, we can't prove you didn't plant it out there."

"Why would I do that?" Eric stared at his uncle.

Uncle Arnie narrowed his eyes. "To throw suspicion on someone else."

Eric's jaw dropped. "But Lacey was out there with me."

"It would be easy to drop a bullet without her seeing you do it," Arnie answered grimly. "She wasn't watching you the whole time, was she?" He gestured to the rock sitting on his desk. "Or maybe you placed this rock out there."

"But I didn't..." Eric closed his eyes.

"I know you're just trying to help, son." Arnie's voice was gentle. "But leave the investigating to us from now on, okay? It's our job. You might make things worse for yourself—unintentionally, of course, but..." His voice trailed off.

"I'm sorry." Eric replied. His head was aching. "Can I have that aspirin?"

"Of course." Arnie opened a desk drawer and placed a bottle on the desk. He got up and got Eric a cup of water from the cooler in the corner. Gratefully, Eric took two tablets and drank the water. He closed his eyes and rubbed his temples.

"The cop in me has to wonder how much I can believe any of this," Uncle Arnie said as he sat back down. "That might be hard to hear, son, but it's what I have to do."

"I'm telling the truth."

"Eric, I'm going to tell you something off the record. I'm about to talk to you as your uncle, not as the sheriff, okay?" Arnie rubbed his forehead. "Like I said, there are a lot of people in this town—including some people on the city council—who think I'm not investigating this case as aggressively as I should be. They think it's because you're the primary suspect and you're my nephew. They think I'm protecting you." He slammed his fist down on the desk. "I'm not. There's not any evidence you shot Sean Brody, other than he was in your car and you were covered in his blood." He sighed. "We didn't know where the crime scene was, so we haven't been able to look for evidence—the bullet, for example. It went through him. So, we've stalled out—because of your amnesia." He shook his head again. "You see how bad that looks for me? It wouldn't be so bad if you weren't my nephew, but you are."

"I'm sorry," Eric whispered.

"And now here you come, with some little bits of evidence." Uncle Arnie shook his head. "It's going to look—"

"People are always going to think I'm lying about the amnesia." Eric's heart sank. "But I'm not." He leaned forward. "Uncle Arnie, when we were out there, there was no sign of Sean's bike. So, how did Sean get out there?"

"Maybe he rode out there with you."

"Sean rode his bike everywhere, according to Lacey," Eric replied. "And he didn't ask me for a ride—he asked me to *meet* him out there. So, he got out there somehow."

"Lacey Tremayne?" Uncle Arnie said. "Your mother said the two of you broke up."

"She drove me out there just now." Eric shook his head. "I didn't think Mom would, and I wanted to talk to Lacey about Sean, ask her a few things."

"Listen, son, I understand this must be very frustrating for you, and I can see where if I were in your place I'd start asking questions, too. But you have to understand this isn't a game."

"A game?" Eric was startled. "I don't think this is a game."

"Sean was murdered—and if you didn't do it, obviously someone else did," Uncle Arnie went on. He leaned back in his chair and folded his hands behind his head. "You're a *danger* to that person—who knows what you saw out there? Who knows what you knew? *Sean* was a danger to someone, dangerous enough for that person to kill him." He put his elbows on his desk. "So *you* might be in danger. This person has already killed once, Eric."

Eric froze. He remembered the feeling of something buzzing past his face in the woods. He swallowed. "Last night…"

"What?"

"Last night after dinner I went for a walk in the woods." He gulped. "The path behind the fence? I wanted to, I don't know, Chris said we used to go camping up there in the woods, and I guess I thought maybe if I looked around where we camped, I might remember something. While I was out there"—he looked down at his hands—"I heard a gunshot, and something passed by my head."

"What?" Uncle Arnie stared at him. "Why didn't you say something? Why didn't you call me?"

"Because I wasn't sure." He ran his fingers through his hair. "Yeah, at the time it scared me, but I didn't see anyone out there. It might have been nothing."

"You need to let me be the judge of that. Tell me exactly where you were when it happened," Uncle Arnie said, his lips set in a grim line.

"I was standing about a yard or two from the clearing where we used to camp."

"I'll get someone up there this afternoon to take a look around." Uncle Arnie shook his head. "And promise me if something like this happens again, you will let me know. Immediately." He tapped a pencil on the desk. "Eric, I don't want you to be the next victim. If someone shot at you last night—"

A finger of fear traced down the back of Eric's neck. "The killer needs to silence me before I get my memory back," he said slowly. The pressure behind his temples felt like his head was going to explode. His stomach was churning.

Uncle Arnie nodded. "Exactly."

"What should I do?" He couldn't believe it had never occurred to him. He could feel panic rising. He took some deep breaths.

"You might want to just stick around the house for a while. I can talk to your mom and dad, make sure you're never left alone, for one thing. And for another, you need to stop nosing around. That's *my* job."

"Will you find out about Sean's bike?"

"Yes."

Eric rose to go. "And my cell phone. Do you have my cell phone?"

Uncle Arnie shook his head. "No. We combed through the wreckage of your car and the area around it with a fine-tooth comb, but we never found your phone."

Interesting, Eric thought. "And where is my car?"

"Why?"

"I'm just curious," Eric replied. "I thought—well, it might not be a bad idea for me to go take a look at it. I thought it might be a trigger for my memory."

"It's at Joe's Salvage Yard, right outside of town. But there's nothing there to find. Trust me, we went over your car thoroughly. Just promise me one thing."

"Sure."

"If you want to take a look at your car, I'll take you out there." A smile played at the corner of his lips. "I'll pick you up tomorrow morning around nine, okay?"

"Thanks." Eric had his hand on the doorknob when his uncle stopped him. "Yes?"

"Remember what I said, son. Be careful—and try not to ever be alone."

CHAPTER ELEVEN

Try not to ever be alone.

His uncle's words reverberated inside his head as he made his way down the stairs to the first floor. He could feel the fear growing each time the words repeated themselves, like a song stuck on endless loop. The aspirin didn't seem to have worked, either. The pounding in his head seemed to be getting worse. Every step down shot a bolt of agony through his head. By the time he was halfway down the staircase he wished it would just explode and put him out of his misery. He grabbed hold of the railing to steady himself. Each time his head throbbed, his vision went red. Someone brushed past him on their way down, and the clacking of their shoes seemed deafening. He was almost to the bottom of the stairs when his knees buckled. He would have fallen if he hadn't had a death grip on the railing.

"Are you all right?" a woman in her early twenties asked, grabbing on to his arm.

"I'm—I'm okay." He somehow managed to get the words out through the blinding pain. He forced what he hoped was a realistic smile on his face. "Thank you, ma'am."

She held on to his arm as he made it down the last four steps, and steered him over to a bench against the wall. "Stay here," she instructed. "I'll get you a glass of water. Are you sure you're all right? Is there someone I can call for you?"

"Water would be nice," he answered. "But I'll be okay."

Her heels clicked against the floor as she walked over to a water cooler. He closed his eyes and leaned back against the wall.

I shouldn't have told him about the gunshot in the woods the other night. He's going to tell Mom and she is going to absolutely freak out. She's never going to let me out of the house again.

Another bolt of pain shot through his head and he bit his lip to keep from crying out. His eyes filled with tears. He put his head between his knees and tried to focus on his breathing.

The woman's legs came into his line of vision just as the pain passed again. He sat up and wiped at his eyes.

"Here, drink this," she said, holding out a cup of water.

"Thanks," Eric said, taking it from her and downing it in one gulp.

"Are you sure I can't call someone?" the woman asked again. "You really don't look well."

"It's just a really bad headache. I took some aspirin—it's not working yet. I'm meeting a friend at the coffee shop across the street," he added, giving her a weak smile. "Thanks for the water."

She sat down on the steps next to him. "You're Eric Matthews, aren't you?" She smiled back at him. "I haven't seen you in years."

Reflexively he shrank back against the railing. She was wearing a navy blue skirt with a matching blazer and a white silk blouse underneath. Her blond hair was pulled up into a bun and her black-rimmed glasses were slipping down her nose. She didn't seem familiar to him, which of course didn't mean much these days.

"Yes," he said cautiously, glancing back up the stairs to the door to his uncle's office. "Who are you?"

"You don't have to be afraid of me," She smiled at him, patting his leg. She narrowed her eyes as she peered at him more closely. "You really have no idea who I am, do you?"

He shook his head, wondering if he could escape if he needed to, and then cursed himself for being so paranoid.

Try not to ever be alone.

"You really *do* have amnesia, don't you? I was pretty sure you weren't faking—but wow, you poor thing, that must be so rough." She clicked her tongue sympathetically. "I'm Taryn Brody—Sean's older sister."

Eric opened his mouth and shut it again.

Try not to ever be alone.

There was no one at the top of the stairs, and the lobby was empty.

Don't panic, don't panic. He closed his eyes. *She's just being nice.*

"Don't worry, I don't think you killed my brother." She shook her head. "I may not have seen or talked to you in four years, but I don't think you'd changed that much from the sweet boy I remembered." She patted his leg. "My mom, on the other hand—"

He exhaled in relief. "I—I saw your mom. She was here."

"I know, I'm sorry—they called me to come pick her up, try to talk some sense into her." Taryn sighed. "She shouldn't have hit you, Eric," she went on. "Try to cut her some slack, okay? Sean's death—well, she hasn't been the same since then. If she was thinking clearly, she'd know you couldn't have done such a thing. But she isn't, Eric. I've been trying to get her into grief counseling, but she just won't do it." She choked up a bit and blinked rapidly, as though trying to stop tears.

"I was trying to save him." Eric's eyes welled up with tears. "I remember that much." He wiped at his eyes. *Don't cry in front of her*, he ordered himself.

"Of course you were." Taryn shook her head again, giving him a reassuring smile. "I mean, I might be only a first-year law student, but even I can see the flaws in the case against you."

"Really?" He turned and looked at her.

"Oh, yeah." She started ticking things off on her fingers. "First, where's the gun? Second, why was Sean in the backseat of your car if you'd shot him? Why would you put him in your car? Third, where were you both at?" She shook her head. "Even I could punch enough holes in the case to get you acquitted, if it came to that. I've tried to explain all this to my mother, but—" She shrugged. "I don't know, it's like this obsession she has about you is what's holding her together. She wasn't like this when Dad died."

"Were you and Sean close?" Eric leaned back against the railing.

"I'd like to think so, but since I started law school last year...I'm afraid I haven't seen him much. But he was acting strange, I thought—a lot different than when I came home for spring break."

"Strange? What do you mean?" Eric watched her face.

"I don't know—secretive, maybe?" She wrinkled her forehead. "Like there was something going on he was worried about? I can't really explain it better than that. I tried to get him to talk to me, but he wouldn't."

He heard Chris sneering *he was a fag* in his head. "Taryn, do you know"—he hesitated, not sure if he should ask—"if Sean was gay?"

"Gay?" She looked startled, and then her face relaxed a bit.

"Hmmm, that *would* make sense, I suppose. I remember thinking he might have a girlfriend he was keeping secret, you know? He used to get phone calls on his cell, and texts all the time—and he would always leave the room when his phone beeped—even went outside. I even asked Mom about it—but she thought I was imagining the whole thing. 'He's just a normal teenager who wants his privacy,' is what she said—she said I was the same way when I was his age." She scratched her forehead. "But if he was gay—that might explain it."

"But he never said anything to you?"

She shook her head. "No—" Her eyes widened. "Oh, my God."

"What?"

"He asked me a lot of questions after that kid in Oakhurst killed himself—the one who was being bullied for being gay," she half whispered. "How could I have been so stupid? He asked if the kids who bullied him could be prosecuted. I thought," she laughed bitterly, "I thought he was asking because—" She bit her lip. "Because he and his friends might be bullying someone." She looked up at the ceiling. "How could I have been so stupid? So blind? I even thought—"

"What?"

"I thought maybe the kid he'd been bullying might have killed him."

Eric swallowed. *If she knew I was the bully…*

I can't go on like this anymore. We need to talk.

Sean's Facebook message—it made sense to him now.

Sean wanted him to stop it, to leave him alone.

The kid in Oakhurst killed himself—what did Lacey say his name was? Paul Benson? Did I push Sean to the point where he thought about killing himself?

But that doesn't explain who killed him.

He changed the subject quickly. "Do you know what happened to Sean's bike?"

"His bike? No, I suppose it's in the garage. Why?"

"Would you mind checking and calling me to let me know?" Eric pushed himself up to his feet.

"Yeah, sure, I'll do it when I get Mom home."

"How was Sean that morning?" Eric asked. He took a deep breath. The pain in his ribs was subsiding. "How was he acting?"

"I didn't see him that morning," Taryn replied. "I'm interning at a firm here in town this summer and I'm doing a lot of research on—" She broke off with a laugh. "You don't care about that, I'm sure. But no, I left before he got up that morning. I didn't see him." Her eyes welled up with tears. "I didn't get a chance—" Her voice choked off with a sob.

"I'm so sorry." Eric touched her shoulder.

"Thanks." She wiped at her eyes and stood up. "I'd better go check on Mom. But if there's anything I can do to help—"

Eric forced a smile. "Thanks. I appreciate it. I'm meeting a friend at the coffee shop and she's probably wondering what's taking me so long. But thank you—thank you for talking to me, and thank you for—for believing me."

"Of course." She stood, and impulsively hugged him. "I'll check on the bike and let you know."

Eric watched her walk up the stairs.

I bullied Sean.

He took a deep breath and started walking out of the building.

Thoughts kept crowding through his mind, horrible thoughts.

I made his life miserable. He was one of my best friends and I turned on him, bullied him, probably pushed him to the point of suicide. You are a horrible person, Eric. A horrible person. If anyone should be dead, it's you. What kind of a person are you? Did it make you feel like a big man to pick on Sean?

His ribs began aching, and his breathing became shallower.

I can't go on this way anymore. This has to stop. Meet me at the Ledge at eleven.

Spots danced in front of his eyes.

He somehow managed to make it out of the building before he had to sit down again.

He sank down on the stairs and put his head down, trying to breathe.

"Thanks for meeting me out here," Sean said, frowning. "We need to talk."

"We could have talked in town," Eric replied. *It was hot out there on the Ledge. The sun was shining directly on them, and he wiped sweat off his forehead. There was no wind. Everything was completely still.*

And he had this weird feeling someone was watching them.

He shifted nervously from one foot to the other.

Sean shook his head. "No, we couldn't," *he said, his voice quiet.* "I'm in real trouble, Eric—but you know that. You've got to help me."

"Why?" *Eric replied.* "You know what you're doing is wrong, Sean. You've got to stop."

"Easy for you to say!" *Sean's voice rose.* "You don't know! You don't have the slightest idea!" *There was a note of hysteria in his voice.* "Just forget about it, and I swear, I'll fix everything."

"Sean—"

Sean started crying. "We used to be friends, Eric." *He*

wiped at his face angrily. "You think you're so damned smart. You think you know everything. But you don't know SHIT, Eric." *He took a step closer. "You believed Chris, didn't you? Well, Chris lied. You never even gave me a chance to explain, to tell you my side of the story." His face twisted in a sneer. "You know Chris and I have been together ever since then, right?"*

"What does that have to do with anything? You're changing the subject—and I thought you wanted to talk about—"

The memory faded.

"Damn it," he swore under his breath.

The pain in his ribs was fading.

He got to his feet, his mind racing.

Chris lied to me. He and Sean were—

He grabbed the railing. *Admit it. Sean and Chris were lovers. Chris is gay.*

Then why did he sleep with Lacey? Does SHE know?

Trembling, he walked down the steps.

Lost in thought, he walked out into the street.

"LOOK OUT!" someone shouted.

He looked to his right and saw a large blue truck barreling down on him.

Oh my God, he isn't slowing down.

He leaped out of the way, barely missing a parked car as the truck roared past. It was so close he could have reached out and touched it.

My God, he thought as his vision started going gray around the edges. He was hyperventilating, and he bent over and put his hands on his knees.

I could have been killed.

Again.

I shouldn't be alive.

Karly's words whispered through his mind again. *You were always a sleeping angel, Eric. God has a plan for you.*

"Are you all right?" a man asked. "What an idiot! He didn't even slow down!"

Eric took a few deep breaths as adrenaline raced through him. "I'm fine," he said, straightening up. "Thanks for yelling."

"People like that shouldn't be allowed to drive," the man went on. "Are you sure you're okay?"

Eric nodded. "Thanks again," he said, and walked up onto the sidewalk. He stopped and bent over, putting his hands on his knees, taking some deep breaths.

The memory didn't make any sense.

Once his heart rate had slowed down again, he straightened up.

Mr. Java was a small place with big plate glass windows with a coffee cup painted on one of them with a smiley face on it. There was a dry cleaner's on the right, and a small liquor store on the other side. The big windows were covered in signs so he couldn't really see inside. He pushed the door open and a bell rang. He paused. It was crowded inside—every booth and table taken. A table of girls near the door stopped talking and looked at him, then started whispering amongst themselves. He lifted his chin and walked in. Lacey stood up from a booth near the back and waved to him.

He walked to the back of the shop and slid into the booth across from her, his back to the door. She smiled. "They're on their way—and with you sitting there, they won't see you until it's too late for them to leave." Her smile faded. "Are you okay?"

"Yeah." he replied, "I almost got hit by a car on the way over here—but give me a minute, I'll be fine."

"Oh my God." Her hand flew to her mouth. "What kind of a car?"

"A blue truck," he replied, thinking, *like Coach Walton's—or like Chris's.*

Could it have been—

"I'll get you a coffee." She stood up and walked over to the counter, returning a few moments later with an iced drink. She set it down in front of him. "Iced mocha, your favorite," she said as she slid back into the booth.

"Thanks."

"How'd it go with your uncle?"

"He's going to check into Sean's bike, so there's no need for you to bother Mrs. Brody. They didn't find my cell phone—it's missing."

"What's the big deal about your cell phone?" Lacey frowned. "I mean, it's annoying not to have one, but can't your mom get you a new one?"

"That isn't it." Eric sighed. "I can't explain it—but I just have this feeling that my phone is somehow important. And it's weird they haven't found it, don't you think? Shouldn't it have been on me, or in my car?"

Her eyes opened wide. "You think the killer took it?"

He nodded. "I think so. And if he did, then there was a reason. Why would he take my phone?" He shook his head. "I don't even know what kind of phone I had."

"You had an iPhone, like mine." She pulled her phone out of her purse and placed it on the table.

He picked her phone up. It was in a pink rubber case, and as he looked at the little symbols on its face, there was one that was a square with a round black circle colored blue on the inside with the word *camera* written underneath it—

—and he was standing in the dark, his heart pounding in his

chest so hard it seemed like it might burst out through his ribs. "No one's going to believe this," he thought, pulling his phone out of his pocket. He clicked on the camera application.

The memory faded.

Damn it, he thought angrily. He took a sip of his drink.

"I also ran into Sean's mom," he said, quickly telling her about his encounters with Mrs. Brody and Taryn.

"Oh, Eric, I'm so sorry." She sighed. "I feel so sorry for Mrs. Brody. She's really had it rough, you know."

"Actually, I don't."

"I'm sorry." She looked stricken.

"It's okay, Lacey. How has she had it rough?"

"Well, Mr. Brody was killed in a car accident about five years ago, and she had to take over their business—they own a bar over by the college campus. It's been really hard on her, and now Sean—I can't imagine how awful this has been for her."

He took a sip of his drink. "I need to ask you something," he said in a quiet voice. "You said the morning I left town we had a big fight, about that kid in Oakhurst who killed himself."

She nodded. "Yeah, we did." She sipped at her drink.

"You said it was because I bullied Sean," he said carefully, not able to meet her eyes.

"You were upset," Lacey replied. "I picked you up and we went out for lunch—we went to the Dairy Queen. You were really shook up, and it surprised me, you know? I mean, it wasn't like you *knew* him or anything. But you just kept talking about how terrible it was—and I said, 'Well, what you guys do to Sean is just as bad as what those kids in Oakhurst were doing to Paul Benson.'"

"I guess I didn't take that too well?"

Lacey laughed. "No, you didn't. That's when we started fighting. You kept insisting it wasn't the same thing." She glanced up as the bell at the front door rang. "There they are," Lacey stood up and waved. "Move over," she whispered, sliding into the booth next to him.

Eric stared at his hands. *What kind of person was I?*

"What is he doing here?" Bob demanded when they walked up to the table.

"Just sit down," Lacey commanded. "We want to talk to you both."

"There's nothing to talk about." Bob was a tall, skinny guy with braces on his teeth and olive skin. His green eyes flashed angrily. "I can't believe you'd pull something like this, Lacey. I might have known. Come on, Kerry, let's get out of here."

"It won't kill us to talk to him," Kerry said, sliding into the booth across from Eric and Lacey. He was shorter than Bob. He had a mop of bluish black curls framing a cherubic face. He put his hands on the table. "Besides, I want to hear what he has to say."

His lips pressed tightly together, Bob sat down next to him. "Okay, so talk." He drummed his fingertips on the table.

"Bob," Lacey said, putting her hand on top of his, "I know Sean was your friend. But Eric didn't kill him, and we both need your help."

Kerry answered, "What do you want?"

Eric bit his lip. "Did either of you see or talk to Sean the morning he died?"

"I did," Bob replied.

"How did he seem?"

"He didn't seem like he was about to be murdered. He was in a really good mood, excited."

"What about?"

"He didn't say," Bob went on. "But—"

"He'd been acting weird for about a week or so," Kerry

finished. "He didn't want to hang out or anything, he seemed really worried about something."

Bob nodded. "That's true—so I was kind of surprised he was in such a good mood that morning." He swallowed. "We made plans to go see a movie later on." His voice thickened. "Needless to say, he didn't show."

"Something was going on with him, but we didn't know what it was," Kerry said. "It was more than just that week, Bob. It had been months. He'd been acting weird for a while."

"What do you mean?" Lacey asked, putting her hand over Eric's.

Bob gave Kerry a dirty look, which he ignored. "Sean never had any money—you know his mom was barely getting by, and he had to help out with the bar all the time, which he really hated. Then all of a sudden a couple of months ago, he had money. He was always treating us to stuff, right, Bob? You thought it was strange, too, remember?"

Bob just nodded.

"Where did the money come from?"

Kerry shook his head. "He would never say—he'd just say not to worry about it."

Eric glanced at Lacey, took a deep breath, and said, "Did Sean have a boyfriend?"

Bob slammed his hands down on the table. "That's it!" His voice rose. "I can't believe you. You and your buddies made his life miserable when he was alive. And you can't even let it rest when he'd dead. You make me *sick*." He started to get up. "Go to hell, Eric."

"Bob, sit down," Kerry ordered.

"Kerry—"

"I said shut up and sit down." Kerry gave him a look, and Bob reluctantly sat back down. "Now that he's dead"—he choked up for a moment, than gathered himself—"I guess it doesn't matter anymore. Yes, Sean was gay, and yes, he was seeing someone."

Bob's eyes goggled. "Kerry—"

"He knew how you'd react so he didn't want you to know." Kerry didn't look at Bob. "But he knew my uncle is gay, so he felt like he could confide in me. Yes, he was seeing someone—he had been for years, but he would never tell me who it was."

Chris, Eric thought. He closed his eyes. "Did either of you know he was going out to the Ledge that morning?"

They both shook their heads.

"Do you know if he knew Paul Benson?"

"Paul Benson?" Bob looked startled. "The kid who committed suicide in Oakhurst?" He tilted his head to one side. "Oh, I see." He mused for a moment. "He was acting weird the week before—before. Yeah, it was after the kid killed himself."

"You think that might have been Sean's boyfriend?" Kerry shook his head, his curls bouncing. "No way. How would they have met?"

"Online, maybe?" Lacey asked.

"Yeah," Bob replied.

"It's possible," Kerry said slowly. "But I think he would have said something to me about it, you know? And I always got the impression the guy he was seeing was local. He didn't have a car—and Oakhurst is too far for him to get by bike."

"Thanks, guys, I appreciate it," Eric said. "And I'm sorry about Sean. I still don't remember what happened, or why we were out there at the Ledge that day, but I didn't shoot him. That much I remember."

"How convenient," Bob said without looking at him.

"Thanks, guys—I'm sorry I had to lie to you," Lacey said as she and Eric stood. "But you wouldn't have come if I told you the truth."

They turned to go, but Bob stopped them. "Eric—"

Eric and Lacey both turned back to the table.

"I *want* to believe you," Bob said brokenly, his eyes welling with tears. "But Sean was such a great guy—and…" His voice trailed off. "You guys were so *awful* to him."

Eric just nodded, and they walked out of the coffee shop.

CHAPTER TWELVE

"Who all used to bully Sean?" Eric asked as she drove him home. "Besides me? Bob and Kerry kept saying *you guys*."

Lacey gripped the steering wheel tightly, her knuckles turning white. "Well, you and Bobby Wheeler and Jemal Washington and Jeremy Glass were the worst," she said finally. "When you guys were together, and Sean was around—" She shook her head. "I used to get so mad at you."

"You didn't mention Chris." Eric looked out the window. He heard Sean's voice again, *Chris and I have been together.*

"Chris never said or did anything, but he never tried to stop you guys, either," she replied in a tight voice. "Which is just as bad. I don't know why you guys were so mean. Sean was such a sweet guy." Her voice broke. "He didn't deserve it. No one does."

Eric closed his eyes and rubbed his forehead. "No," he finally said. "I'm—I'm so *ashamed* of myself."

"You guys thought it was *funny*." Her voice cut him like a knife, and in a gentler voice, she added, "I don't think you guys ever thought about how it felt, you know? I think you did realize, though, after—" She paused. "It really rattled you, Eric. I was kind of a bitch to you."

"But I must not have stopped doing it," he mumbled. "That had to be what Sean's message was about. I think—I think I have to face up to…" But he couldn't bring himself to say it.

"What?"

"Maybe after I got Sean's message…" He took a deep breath. "Maybe I told someone, one of the other guys about it. And maybe—"

Lacey pulled the car over, and he jerked against his seat belt as the car stopped. "You think you might have set him up?" Her voice quivered.

He couldn't look at her.

She started crying softly.

"That would make me just as guilty as if I pulled the trigger." He wanted her to tell him it wasn't possible, he would never do such a thing.

But all she did was keep crying.

They sat in silence for a few moments until she pulled herself together. "I don't believe that for a minute," she finally said. "You *might* have set him up—but not to get killed." She pulled back onto the street. "I don't think you would have done that, not after what happened to Paul Benson. It really upset you, Eric. I don't think you would have done that."

"Thanks," he murmured, still unable to look at her.

She turned down his street. "If one of the guys killed Sean, Eric, you didn't know it was going to happen. You have to believe that."

"I don't know what to believe anymore. Maybe the reason I don't remember is because I don't *want* to remember. Dr. Weston said that some people experience that kind of amnesia— their mind trying to protect them from some horrible traumatic memory. Maybe that's what's happening to me."

"You don't know that," she whispered.

"Who knows?"

Eric's mother was pacing on the porch when they pulled into the driveway.

"That doesn't look good," Lacey said as she put the car in park. "I've seen your mom like that before. You want me to stick around?"

Eric smiled weakly. "No, I think I can handle it."

"You're sure? I don't mind."

"I'm sure. Thanks, Lacey." Eric hesitated for a moment before leaning over and kissing her on the cheek. "I appreciate all your help today."

"Was glad to do it, Eric." She smiled. "Anytime you need me, you just call me, okay? I—" She hesitated. "I still love you."

Eric didn't know what to say. Conflicting thoughts crowded through his mind—*say it back, it's not fair to lead her on, it won't kill you to say it back, I don't know how I feel*—and the silence got awkward.

Lacey laughed and touched the side of his face. "It's okay, Eric. I know the situation, and I'm fine with it. I do still love you. Now go on, your mom's still pacing—and the longer she paces, the more wound up she'll be."

Eric got out of the car and waved as she drove off. *She's really a great girl*, he thought as he turned and watched his mother pacing. She stopped and folded her arms, her foot tapping. *Time to face the music.* He walked up to the porch.

"Thank God you're all right!" Mom's voice quivered as she bounded across the porch and smothered him in a hug. "Why didn't you tell me you were going to see Arnie? I would have gone with you. You shouldn't have gone there without me or your father, you know." She let go and wiped at her eyes. "And why didn't you tell me someone *shot* at you last night?" She wiped at her eyes.

"Because I wasn't sure," Eric replied, walking in the front door with her at his heels. "And I didn't want to worry you or Dad when there wasn't a reason to." He shook his head. "Uncle Arnie shouldn't have said anything to you. It could have been nothing. I shouldn't have said anything to him."

"Eric, if Arnie thought it was nothing, why does he have two people out there in the woods looking around?" She grabbed his wrists and stepped closer. "I don't care. Maybe it was nothing. But you can't keep stuff like that from us, honey." Her voice broke.

"Someone fired a gun in the woods, Mom. It could have been anything. A hunter, maybe. Some kids screwing around. Maybe someone shooting at targets for practice." *If it was nothing, then what was it that flew by so close to your head?*

"Still. We almost lost you once—I don't want…" Her voice shook, but she seemed to gather herself before continuing. "If *anything* like that happens again—I don't care if you think it's nothing, you need to tell me. Is that understood?"

He nodded, but decided not to say anything about the blue truck.

"Arnie told me about Gina Brody," she went on, her lip curling. "I've already told him to go ahead and press charges." She folded her arms. "How dare she lay a hand on you! I've a good mind to sue her."

"Mom, don't." Eric felt tired. "She's lost her son already. Don't do this. I'm okay, really. She didn't hurt me or anything."

"And I almost lost *my* son. She'd better be damned grateful I wasn't there. I'd have torn her throat out with my bare hands." Her lips compressed together into a tight line. "I still might."

"Mom—"

"I'm so sorry that happened to you." Mom's eyes welled up with tears. "And I don't think you should leave the house anymore."

"I can't stay inside all day every day for the rest of my life, Mom." Eric sighed, thinking, *I knew I shouldn't have said anything.*

But at least Bob and Kerry agreed to help out, he reminded himself. *That's something.*

"And I don't want you talking about any of this to your uncle without a lawyer," she went on. "I know he's family, Eric, but you can't put him in the middle of all of this—and it's his *job*." Her eyebrows knit together. "But it's going to be a long time before I let him set foot in this house again."

"But Mom—" He paused. "When I start remembering, I *have* to tell the police. They have to catch the guy who killed Sean. If I don't, he might get away with it."

She went on like he hadn't said anything. "Tom Castleberry from the country club is a lawyer. I'll give him a call and maybe he can recommend someone."

"Mom—"

She started pacing around the living room, still talking. Her voice was low and quiet, more like she was thinking out loud than talking to him. Her hands were shaking as she walked.

He got up and walked upstairs, leaving her to it. When he reached his room, he collapsed onto the bed and stared at the ceiling.

He put his hands behind his head and closed his eyes.

The blue truck—that might not have been anything either. But both Chris and Coach Walton drove blue trucks. And if his memory was right, Chris and Sean had been sneaking around together for years.

Could Chris have tried to kill him?

The truck had sped up instead of slowing down, he wasn't wrong about that. He'd heard the engine rev—that was why he'd turned and seen it coming.

I wish I'd gotten a better look at the truck, he chided himself. He sighed and got up, walking over to his desk.

An iPhone was plugged into his computer.

He unplugged it and stared at it. "This can't be my old phone," he said out loud.

"Mom got you a new one today," Danny said from the doorway. "She had me sync it with your computer. It's all charged and ready to go. All your contacts and everything reloaded from your computer."

"Thanks," Eric replied. He clicked on the Contacts icon. A list of alphabetized names came up. He scrolled through, not recognizing most of them. When he got to Chris's name, he touched the screen.

"Danny, how well did you know Sean?" he asked as he touched the Text Message command. He sat back down on the bed.

Danny shrugged. "Hardly at all. He used to hang out here when I was little, but I didn't know him at all. He was always nice to me—which is more than I can say for Chris." He scowled. "Chris is an asshole."

"Can I ask you something else?"

"Sure—it's not like I can stop you."

"Why would I care if Sean was gay? Would it have mattered to me?"

Danny stared at him, his mouth open. "You and your friends used to pick on him all the time," he said slowly. "You used to call him *fag*. It was your favorite insult—you used to call me that all the time. 'Don't be such a little fag, Danny.'" Danny laughed. It sounded unpleasant. "I don't know how Sean stood it."

He heard Karly's voice in his head. *There was more to you than the shallow boy most people saw.*

He swallowed. "I'm really sorry about everything, Danny."

That surprised Danny. He looked down at the floor and mumbled, "Well, you should be. It's so hard being your brother." His eyes glittered with tears. "You're so perfect."

He had started typing a text to Chris, but he stopped and looked at his brother. "What do you mean?"

Danny rolled his eyes. "Please. Everyone compares me to you, you know, everyone—even Mom and Dad. 'Why can't you be more like your brother?'" He mimicked their mother's voice perfectly. "I get it, already—you're perfect and I'm not." His chin trembled. "It's not my fault. I try, really, I do. But nothing I do is ever good enough."

"I'm sorry, Danny. That's just wrong." Eric's heart broke a little as he looked at his little brother. "People shouldn't do that. And I'm not perfect." He gave a bitter laugh. "I'm finding out just how awful I really am. God, what was wrong with me?"

Danny opened his mouth to say something, but closed it again.

Overwhelmed, Eric felt tears rising in his own eyes and blinked them back. *Did I set Sean up to be killed?*

Danny sat down on the bed next to him and put his arm around him. "Don't cry, Eric," Danny said, his own voice trembling. "You weren't that bad, really."

"Wasn't I?" Eric replied, "You thought I killed Sean. My own brother."

"I don't think that," Danny said. "I don't. You're my brother. I love you, Eric. I was just mad. I'm sorry. I shouldn't have said it. I didn't mean it."

Eric looked at him and smiled weakly. He wiped at his eyes. "You didn't?"

Danny shook his head. "Uh-uh." He sniffed, and wiped at his own eyes.

"Thanks." Eric hugged him.

"Mom says someone shot at you last night," Danny said. "Really?"

"I don't know if someone actually shot at me," Eric replied with a shrug. "I went out into the woods and someone fired a gun. I don't know if they were firing at me or not. Something went by my head, but it could have just been a bug or something." He looked at his brother and forced a laugh. "The only person I can think of who'd want to shoot me is Mrs. Brody."

"Well, it's not like you can remember much," Danny replied. "Are you sure someone fired a gun?"

"I may not remember much, but I remember what a gunshot sounds like," Eric retorted, noticing Danny's face growing paler. "Why?"

Danny licked his lips. "No reason." He began fidgeting.

"Danny?"

"I've got to get ready. We have a game tonight." Danny darted down the hallway.

Eric stared at the empty doorway. *He acted strange after he brought up the gunshot, like he knows something.*

Eric shook his head. That wasn't possible. Danny had been in the house with their parents. He picked up his phone and finished texting Chris: *Hey buddy, I need to talk to you. Can you come over?* He put the phone down on the bed and walked over to his computer. He pulled up the Internet browser. He typed in *Paul Benson suicide Oakhurst.*

His computer hummed, and a page of links came up. He clicked on the one from the Oakhurst paper.

The page loaded.

LOCAL HIGH SCHOOL STUDENT COMMITS SUICIDE
WAS CONSTANT BULLYING THE REASON?

There was a picture of him. He was smiling at the camera. He was a nice enough looking kid, with dark brown hair and glasses. There was a gap between his front two teeth.

There was something *familiar* about him.

"Hey fag!" someone shouted, and a milkshake flew through the air. It hit the kid square in the face, and it exploded, covering him with chocolate milkshake, soaking into his hair and shirt, running down his face.

There was an explosion of laughter.

His phone clanged, startling him. He picked it up. There was a message from Chris: *Sure bud, can be there in a few.*

He turned back to his computer and stared at the kid's picture. Yes, he could remember the kid, with chocolate milkshake all over him. *Where were we? Where did this happen? Who threw the milkshake at him? Was it me?*

He started reading the article.

> *OAKHURST (Reuters) A 17-year-old boy hanged himself last evening in the garage of his family home in an apparent suicide, local police said.*
>
> *The boy, Paul Benson, was a junior at Oakhurst High School. Friends claim Benson was being bullied, and had been for years. Karen Davidek, 17, said the harassment had been going on since junior high school. "He couldn't even walk to class without someone calling him names or knocking his books out of his hands," she said between sobs. "And the teachers didn't do*

anything about it. They saw it happen and did nothing. They acted like he deserved it, for being different."

His phone rang. The caller was unidentified. "Hello?"

"Hi, Eric, this is Taryn Brody." She sounded like she'd been crying. "I just got home. They didn't press charges after all."

"I told them not to."

"I know." She blew out her breath. "Maybe a night in jail would be good for her, I don't know. Anyway, I wanted to let you know Sean's bike is in the garage."

"It is?" *So, how did Sean get out to the Ledge that day?*

She sighed. "Yeah, it's where it always is, right by the garbage cans inside the garage door." Her voice broke. "It's got cobwebs on it now, and it's getting dusty. I'm sorry—but I can see him riding it—"

"Thanks, Taryn, for checking. And thanks for being so nice to me this afternoon." He closed his eyes. "If there's anything I can do to help..."

"Thanks, that's sweet of you, but I better go check on Mom." She hung up.

He tossed the phone onto the bed and stared at his computer screen.

He couldn't read any more of the article, so he closed the browser. He opened a Word document and typed, *How did Sean get out to the Ledge that day?* After a few moments, he added, *Why did Sean want to meet me out there? Where did Sean's money come from? What was he worried about the last week or so he was alive? And where is SEAN's cell phone—and mine? Does it make any sense that neither one of us had our cell phones ON us?*

It didn't make any sense. Even if their phones didn't work out at the Ledge, they would have had them in their pockets.

He bit down on his lip, hard enough to make his eyes water.

The only person who might know some of the answers was Chris.

Chris had lied about what happened on the campout.

What else had he lied about?

It seemed to take forever before he heard a car pull into the driveway. He looked out the window and saw Chris getting out of his blue truck. He was wearing long basketball shorts and a T-shirt. He sauntered to the porch, and Eric heard the doorbell ring.

A few minutes later Chris was in his doorway. "Hey, buddy, what's up?"

"Come on in." Eric forced a smile on his face. Chris sat down on the bed. Eric shut the bedroom door.

"Why'd you shut the door?" Chris grinned. "What's going on?"

"I don't want anyone to hear what we're talking about." Eric sat down in his desk chair. "Chris, why did you lie to me?"

His grin didn't waver. "What are you talking about?"

"You lied about what happened when we went camping in the eighth grade. With Sean."

Chris's smile faded. "What are you talking about?"

"Why did you lie to me, Chris?" Eric watched his face. "I remembered something, Chris. Sean told me about you two."

Chris looked down at his hands. "Dude, I—"

"How long were you and Sean involved?" Eric interrupted. "And why didn't you tell me? Why did you lie about what happened on the campout?"

"I couldn't risk it." Chris looked at him, his face flushed. "You don't remember. You don't know what my dad is like, do you? You can't remember?"

Eric shook his head. "What does your dad have to do with it?"

"My dad would kill me if he knew. He hates gay people, says they're an abomination. So when you woke up and caught us, all I could think was you'd tell my dad, and so I decided to—"

"Blame it all on Sean and make me hate him," Eric finished. He felt ill. He couldn't look at Chris. "But he forgave you, didn't he? And you two have been, *were*—ever since?"

Chris got up and walked over to the window. "He didn't forgive me at first, no. It took a while. I didn't know when it happened you were going to tell people about Sean, were going to make his life miserable." Chris's voice shook. "And then I couldn't be honest with you. I saw what Sean was going through, thanks to you. And I didn't want that to happen to me." He pounded on the wall with his fist. "Sean was so great, such a great guy—you had no idea." He barked out a bitter laugh. "He didn't care. He didn't care that you guys called him names and picked on him. He didn't care that people avoided him because they didn't want to get the same treatment. God, he was so brave."

"You loved him," Eric said, closing his eyes.

"Of course I loved him." Chris shook his head. "I couldn't stand to watch it, you know? And whenever I was about to say something, he'd just look at me and shake his head. I was such a coward—maybe he'd still be alive if…" He turned back around. "The funny thing was, you didn't have anything against gay people. You just thought you were being funny." He scoffed. "You have no idea how many times I just wanted to punch you."

"Why would you even want to be friends with me?"

"What choice did I have?" Chris's voice rose. "I had to go on pretending to be someone I wasn't. What was I supposed to do? The best thing I could hope for from my dad was he'd just throw me out. Not much of a choice there, was there? And Sean," his eyes filled with tears, "Sean didn't want me to have to deal with it. He just kept reminding me it was only one more year, and then we could go off to college and get away from my dad, away from Woodbridge, and start our lives over and be together. He kept telling me to keep it secret, even when I got so fed up with all the lies I didn't care anymore..."

"My God, I was such a horrible person." Eric felt like throwing up. His stomach was churning.

"You don't know the half of it. Remember Paul Benson? No, of course not, you don't remember anything, do you?"

"Paul Benson," Eric breathed.

"Sean and I met him on a chat site for gay teens," Chris spat the words out. "He had it rough, he was suffering so much. So, Sean and I decided to go meet him, talk to him, let him know he wasn't alone." He looked back out the window. "How were we supposed to know you and Jemal and a couple of other guys would get bored and drive over to Oakhurst?"

Eric's heart sank.

"We were supposed to meet him at McDonald's," Chris went on. "But when we got there, guess who was already there?" He turned around and glared at Eric. "There you all were, surrounding him, laughing at him. He was covered in milkshake and crying." He took a deep breath. "I wanted to stop it, but Sean wouldn't let me—he reminded me of what would—would *happen* if we showed up there, him with me, and came to Paul's defense. So we didn't even stop. We just came back home." His voice broke. "He hanged himself that night, Eric." A tear ran down his right cheek. "And I have to live with it. Knowing that if I hadn't been such a *fucking* coward, we might have saved him."

It was my fault, Eric thought, *Paul Benson killed himself because of me.* There was a roaring in his ears. He tried to speak but he couldn't.

"That night at the party, I wasn't drunk," Chris went on. "Lacey was, sure, but I wasn't. When I saw her—all I could think about was how I couldn't bring Sean as my date. And I thought about what you'd done to Sean—and me—and Paul… and I wanted to punish you. But it didn't bring Paul back."

"Oh, God," Eric whispered. "You really must hate me."

"That's the funny thing." Chris turned back from the window, leaning against the sill. "I don't hate you, Eric. I should but I don't. See, that's part of it, too." He wiped at his eyes. "If I hadn't lied to you, if I hadn't been such a coward back in the eighth grade, or any time since then, *none* of this would have happened."

Eric wanted to give him a hug, but stayed on the bed. "You loved Sean."

Chris nodded as he wiped at his eyes.

"Then help me find out who killed him. It's how we can make this right. And I'm so sorry, Chris. So very sorry."

Chris nodded.

"Bob and Kerry said Sean came into some money the last few months," Eric went on. "Do you know from where?"

Chris nodded, wiping at his eyes. "He was—he was selling drugs." His voice broke. "Someone found out about us, and threatened to tell everyone if he didn't do it. He did it for me." He covered his face with his hands and started sobbing.

"Maybe this is why he was killed, Chris," Eric said softly. "Did he tell you why he wanted to talk to me out at the Ledge that morning?"

Chris shook his head. "I didn't even know he was going out there. I would have given him a ride. But the night before, he told me he was going to put a stop to it all." He choked up again. "And then the next day he was dead. I wondered—I wondered if you were the one making him sell the drugs. He hated drugs, absolutely hated them. He hated what he was doing."

Eric got up and crossed the room. "I'm so sorry, Chris."

"Thanks." Chris gave him a weak smile. "Is there anything else you wanted to know?"

Eric shook his head.

"It's funny—now that I've gotten that all out, I feel better. I need to—to go be by myself. I need to think." Chris stopped at the door and looked back. "I can't keep this up, this lying. Paul and Sean—well, they'd still be alive if I weren't such a coward."

"Don't do that to yourself, Chris." Eric wiped at his own eyes. "If you need anything—or just to talk, call me, okay?"

"Thanks."

The door closed behind him.

CHAPTER THIRTEEN

So, Sean and Chris had been lovers.

My God, what a monster I was. I drove that kid to suicide. Eric berated himself as he walked over to the window. He watched Chris get into his truck and back out of the driveway. *My best friend couldn't be honest with me because he thought I'd turn on him.*

"You've been a lousy brother and friend," he said out loud, getting his laptop and walking back over to the bed. He stretched out and opened the computer. He clicked on the Internet icon and waited for Facebook to load.

He stared at the photo of himself he'd loaded for his profile picture, the smiling face in the football uniform.

He sighed.

He opened the message page and looked at Sean's final message.

"Why?" he whispered. "Why did you want me to meet you? And why did I go?"

From everything he'd learned, there was absolutely no reason he would have ever agreed to meet Sean anywhere—much less out at the Ledge.

The memory you had of taking the picture with your phone.

"That must have been it," he thought, cursing himself again for not being able to remember more.

He closed his eyes and leaned back against the pillows. He tried clearing his mind, the way Dr. Weston had suggested, and imagined himself in a peaceful place. He concentrated on his breathing, making sure his breaths were deep and long both in and out.

After a few moments, he began to feel really calm and didn't have to think about the breathing pattern anymore.

And he felt his mind starting to drift.

Sean was standing in front of a locker, digging through the clutter in the top part. He got closer. The hall was full of noise— talking, laughing, students were everywhere—and he just kept drawing closer and closer to Sean.

He felt the contempt, the dislike, rising inside him. Sean was wearing a turquoise pullover shirt with a collar and a pair of loose-fitting jeans. His shoulder-length blondish hair curled upward slightly at the bottom.

He shoved him in the back, and Sean stumbled forward a little bit. He turned around. "What's your problem, Eric? Why can't you just leave me alone?"

"I don't like fags."

Sean just stared back, not saying anything, not blinking. He closed his locker. "I can't believe we were ever friends."

"You and me both, fag."

"What happened to you? You used to be a nice guy." Sean pushed past him. "The funny thing, Eric, is I feel sorry for you. One day, you're not going to be the star on campus anymore—if there's any justice in this world, you'll have a crappy life. And one day you're going to wake up and look at your life and ask, 'How did I ever wind up like this?' So, I'll save you the headache and tell you now. Because you deserve it. You deserve every

rotten thing that's going to happen to you. I just hope I'm there to see it."

He walked off down the hall.

He sat up on the bed.

"I can't believe I did that," he whispered.

He heard the front door slam shut downstairs, then angry, loud voices shouting at each other. He put his laptop down and walked over to the window. He didn't recognize the car in the driveway. Frowning, he went downstairs.

"You aren't welcome here and you aren't talking to him unless he has a lawyer present." Mom shouted.

"Nancy, there's no need for him to have a lawyer," Uncle Arnie replied in a patient voice. The strain of holding his own temper had flushed his face red. He ran a hand over his scalp. "How many times do I have to tell you? Eric *asked* me to come over and look at his computer."

"I don't care," she spat, her own face turning red, her hands perched on her hips. "I don't care if Christ the Lord told you to come here. You aren't talking to him again unless there's a lawyer in the room. Do you understand? Or do I need to translate into *stupid*?"

Arnie put his hands into his pockets. "Do you want me to get a subpoena, Nancy? Do you really want that?"

"Besides, you already took his computer once. What do you think you're going to find this time?" She started tapping her foot.

Uncle Arnie sighed. "Nancy, Eric wants to show me something he found on his computer. He asked me to come over here. Now, are you going to calm down and act like a human being with a lick of sense, or are you going to keep screaming at me?"

"He doesn't have the final say." Her voice was more subdued, but her face remained red. "Now get out. This is the last time I'm going to tell you."

"Mom," Eric said. She turned and looked at him. There were tears in her eyes. "It's true, Mom. I asked Uncle Arnie to come by."

"Eric, I know you think you're trying to help, but you can't do this." She was actually trembling. "Please don't. Let me call a lawyer and get him over here, son. Please."

"What do you think I'm going to do, Nancy?" Uncle Arnie stared at her. He threw his hands up in the air. "Everybody in town already thinks I'm cutting him a break because he's family! I'm just trying to catch a killer!" He sank down on the couch and buried his face in his hands. "Maybe I ought to just resign and walk away, go back to being a car dealer." He looked up at his sister. "Is that what you want, Nancy? Someone else being sheriff? Someone who isn't going to be as fair as I am? Someone who'll just charge him on the circumstantial evidence and lock him up and throw away the key? Is that what you want?"

She didn't say anything, just stood there staring at him.

"Come on, Uncle Arnie." Eric finally said. "Come on up to my room."

"Eric—"

"Mom, *please*."

The expression on her face almost broke his heart.

"I know you're trying to help," he went on. "I love you, Mom. But I have to do this. It's the right thing." His voice shook a little bit, so he stopped to catch his breath before he continued. "Someone killed Sean. It wasn't me. But if I don't tell Uncle Arnie things that can help him catch the guy because I'm afraid it might make me look bad, well, that's not the kind of person I want to be." He put his arms around her. "Think about poor Mrs. Brody. What if it was *me* who'd been killed—and Sean knew something that could help catch the killer? Would you want Mrs. Brody stopping him from talking to Uncle Arnie?"

"No." She sniffled. "All right. I give up. I can't fight both of you." She pushed away from him and turned to look at her brother. "Go on, then. But I'm warning you, Arnie—"

"All I want is to find out the truth. And if Eric didn't kill Sean, he has nothing to worry about from me. Nancy, you know me better than that."

"I don't know what I know anymore." She shook her head and walked into the kitchen.

"Well, that wasn't quite as bad as I thought it would be," Arnie said with a weary smile when they got to Eric's room. "You handled that really well, son."

"Yeah, well. This has been really hard on her. Dad, too—and Danny. That's why I want this whole thing to be over once and for all." Eric picked up his computer and handed it to his uncle. "Facebook is already loaded."

Arnie put the computer down on the desk and straddled the desk chair. Eric stood behind him, watching as he clicked the message from Sean.

"See? It was Sean's idea," Eric said. "And his bike is in the Brodys' garage—so how did he get out there that day?"

"How do you know that?" Arnie looked back over his shoulder.

"I talked to his sister. His bike is there. So he didn't take it that day to the Ledge, Uncle Arnie. So, someone had to have driven him out there that morning—which means someone else was out there. And his cell phone is missing—and so is mine."

"Did you have it with you that morning?" Arnie asked, turning back to the computer. He clicked on the Profile link, which took him back to Eric's main page. He started scrolling down through the comments posted there.

"I don't remember, Uncle Arnie," Eric replied with a sigh. "But Mom makes Danny take his every time he leaves the house. I can't imagine she wouldn't make me take mine."

"Nobody goes anywhere without their phones anymore," Arnie agreed. He whistled. "Some of these posts are just plain mean-spirited."

"Yeah, well, I don't pay any attention to those." He glanced over his uncle's shoulder. Someone named Bill Shaughnessy had posted *Rot in jail, murderer!* "I don't even know who that is." He laughed bitterly. "What am I saying? I don't know who any of those kids are."

"Well, son, not everyone can be your friend. There's always going to be people who don't like you, no matter how hard you try." Arnie kept scrolling down. He sighed and clicked on the Friends link. "So, you and Sean weren't friends on here?"

"We weren't friends anywhere." Eric walked over to his window and looked out. "That's what I don't get, Uncle Arnie. Chris and Lacey both told me that Sean and I weren't friends, we hadn't been since eighth grade. We didn't talk, we didn't hang out, nothing. So why would he send a message like that? And why would I go meet him? It doesn't make sense, Uncle Arnie. But I don't remember, and apparently the only other person who did know is dead." He banged his head against the windowpane. "If I don't ever remember, we'll never know."

"Eric, the killer knows." Arnie clicked to go back to the message list. "The killer had to know you were both going to be up there."

What scares me the most is the thought maybe I was the one who told the killer—I was the one who got him killed.

His new phone chirped. He picked it up and stared at the message.

Murderer.

The sender was listed as Unknown.

He closed his eyes and moaned.

"Eric?" Arnie got up from the chair. He grabbed the phone out of Eric's hands and stared at the small screen. He swore under his breath. He glanced at Eric. "Are you okay?"

Eric nodded. "You'd think I'd be used to it by now," he said sadly.

Arnie put the phone down and turned back to the computer. "There's just the one message from Sean," he mused aloud. "And you're sure you have no idea what he wanted?"

Eric shook his head. "I keep trying to remember, but nothing seems to work." He felt himself getting frustrated, so he walked over to the bed and sat down. He took a few deep breaths until the feeling passed.

"I don't believe you killed Sean," Arnie said.

Eric opened his eyes. "What?"

"The evidence doesn't really support that theory. Tell me more about the bike."

Eric blew out a sigh of relief. "Sean apparently rode his bike everywhere—he didn't have a car. So, I was curious about how he got out there…his bike wasn't there this morning when Lacey and I were out there. It's possible he got a ride, or his bike was left there and stolen later, so I asked his sister. She checked. The bike's there. So, someone else took him out there. We just don't know who."

Arnie whistled. "Good work, son. Maybe I should deputize you—you're getting a lot further on this than I have." He leaned back in his chair. "Now, who do you suppose took him out there?"

"Whoever it was had to be the killer." Eric was just thinking out loud, but it was actually helping. He walked back over to the window in time to see a big blue truck drive by—slowly.

His heart leapt into his throat, but then the truck turned into a driveway a few houses down and across the street. He shook his head and turned back to face his uncle. "Do you know where Sean was that morning?"

Arnie shook his head. "He was still in bed when the sister went to her office. And he had already left the house by the time Mrs. Brody woke up—she keeps late nights, you know, with the bar and all."

"No one saw him at all that morning?" Eric frowned. "Is that even possible?"

"We haven't found anyone who saw him that morning. Neighbors, friends—no one." Arnie shrugged. "Hard to believe, especially in a town this size, but no one remembers seeing him that morning. Doesn't mean they didn't, they just don't remember."

"I talked to two of his friends after I left your office," Eric said slowly, explaining what Bob and Kerry had said about how Sean suddenly always seemed to have money. "Where was the money coming from? Bob and Kerry didn't know. I believed them, Uncle Arnie."

"Nobody mentioned any of this to me," Arnie replied, irritation creeping into his voice. "And I talked to all of his friends."

"Maybe they didn't think it meant anything. Bob and Kerry were pretty convinced I'd killed him, so the money didn't seem to matter." He laughed. "They still think I killed him—or at least they want to."

"They want to?" Arnie looked puzzled.

"They don't like me very much, Uncle Arnie. And as you saw on my Facebook page, they're not the only ones."

"You seem to be handling this all really well," Arnie said. "I haven't gotten Dr. Guzman's full report yet, but I talked to her. One of the things she mentioned was how remarkably well-adjusted you seemed, how you were handling everything so much better than she could have anticipated." He shook his head. "Better than an adult in the same situation, she thought."

"Did she believe me?"

Arnie nodded. "She believes you are suffering from amnesia."

"Well, that's good." Eric sighed. He rubbed his eyes. "Maybe the reason I am handling this all so well is because I do have amnesia. Apparently—"

"Apparently what?"

"What did you think of me, Uncle Arnie, before all this happened?" Eric ignored his question.

"What?" Arnie looked puzzled. "I thought you were a good kid. Why would you ask that?"

"It's weird, I can't explain." Eric ran his fingers through his hair. "Some of the stuff I'm finding out about me—I don't like. I don't think I was a very good person, Uncle Arnie."

"That's just crazy," Arnie blustered. "You were a good kid. You played sports, got good grades, had a sweet girlfriend—I imagine people were just plain jealous of you."

"I guess," Eric replied, not convinced. "Thanks, Uncle Arnie."

"Glad I could put your mind at ease." Arnie stood up and closed the laptop. "I'll be getting out of here, then. I don't like the thought of you poking around in this, Eric. You've done a good job, I'll grant you that, but I don't want you to ask questions or look around any more. You might be in danger, and the more you nose around the more danger you could be in. You could possibly know the identity of a murderer, son. And someone who's killed before won't draw the line at killing again."

Tell him about the truck, Eric thought.

"Someone may or may not have shot at you in the woods last night—most likely not, but who knows for sure?" Arnie went on. "But I was serious this afternoon when I told you not to go anywhere alone, or be in the house by yourself. Always make sure you're with someone—preferably an adult."

"And I've got this cell phone." Eric held it up again. The screen still read *murderer.* He deleted the message quickly.

"Always have it with you and always have it charged," Arnie went on grimly. "You might want to put nine-one-one on speed dial, so all you have to do is punch a button." He paused at the door. "And I am going to have a talk with your mother before I leave." He wagged his index finger at Eric. "Keep your eyes and ears open—pay attention to everything around you. And I'll check with your phone service to see if I can get the name of the person who sent you that text message. Probably nothing—kids just being kids, I reckon, but it won't hurt to make sure. Now you be careful, you hear me?" He shut the door behind him.

Eric closed his eyes and tried to remember again, but nothing came. After a few more frustrating moments, he got up and walked over to his laptop. He clicked on the Bookmarks icon. "What's this?" he smiled to himself, looking at a bookmark that said *Woodbridge Herald*. He clicked on it, and the website for the town newspaper came up—to a story about him in the sports section from last football season. There was the original of the Facebook profile picture he used. He scanned the article, which made him sound like the perfect teenage boy—football star, dating a cheerleader, straight-A student, would love to play college football but not sure if he had the talent—and rolled his eyes. *No wonder Danny hated me*, he thought, clicking on the Home icon.

He was about to type *sean brody murder* in the search box when a headline caught his eye.

DRUG PROBLEM AT WOODBRIDGE STATE
PART TWO OF A FIVE-PART SERIES
By Maureen Brownworth

Curious, he started reading.

He got to the second paragraph when he froze.

Ecstasy.

And all of a sudden, a memory flashed into his brain.

"Why, Sean?"

"You'd never understand," Sean replied with a sneer. *"What are you going to do now that you know? Turn us into the police?"*

"I don't know what I want to do."

"That's so typical." They were standing in a locker room. *"Why are you even hesitating, Eric? Isn't this what you always wanted? Now you can get rid of Sean the Fag once and for all."*

"I'm just trying to understand."

"What's to understand? Since when do you care anything about me?"

And unbidden, the sight of Lacey's tearstained face flashed through his mind, sobbing, saying, *"I'm sorry"* over and over. *"I'm sorry about everything, Sean,"* he heard himself saying. *"I—I don't know what else to say. I know I can't make anything up to you, but I'm sorry."*

Sean's eyes widened, and he started laughing. *"This is all about your little girlfriend, isn't it?"* he sneered. *"I heard all about it—everyone knows what she did at that party last Friday. I wasn't invited—but everyone knows, Eric. So I guess you know what it feels like now to have a friend turn on you, to become the person everyone whispers about after you walk past? It sucks, doesn't it? And you've only had a little taste of what MY life has been like since junior high! Sean Brody's a fag! Sean Brody's a fag!" he mimicked in a high-pitched voice with a lisp. "Getting your books knocked out of your hands, getting your clothes stolen from your gym locker so everyone can laugh, yeah, it's a great life." His voice shook, his eyes filling with tears. "You were my friend, Eric. My friend. Since we were kids, since kindergarten."*

"I'm sorry. I don't know what else to say. But you've got to stop selling the drugs, Sean. You've got to stop."

Sean shook his head. "That's something else you don't understand, Eric. I can't stop."

"He was dealing ecstasy," Eric said out loud. "And I knew—somehow I found out. That was why he wanted me to go out to the Ledge that day—he wanted to know what I was going to do about it, if I was going to turn him in." He clicked Facebook back open and reread the message.

He felt sick to his stomach.

He could still hear the pain in Sean's voice as he shouted at him in the locker room. Years of hurt and humiliation were in his voice—hurt and humiliation he laid squarely at the feet of his former best friend.

And all that time, Chris and Sean were lovers.

I was such an idiot. And why did it matter if Sean was gay? Why did I care so much? What made me be so mean to him? What was wrong with me? Why was I such an asshole?

There was a knock on the door, and Mom stuck her head in. "You need to get ready." Her voice was subdued.

"For what?"

"Danny's game. Your father's meeting us there—and Arnie made it very clear to me I wasn't to leave you home alone." She folded her arms. "So get a move on."

"Mom—"

"Even if your uncle hadn't said anything, you'd be going

to this game." She tapped her foot. "It means a lot to your brother."

Danny couldn't care less if I was there, how can you not be aware of how much he hates me? "I doubt that."

Mom crossed the room and sat on the edge of his bed. "Eric, listen to me. This is a big game. If we win, we get to go to the playoffs. If we don't, the season is over. I know he doesn't act like it, but your brother *worships* you. If you don't come to the game you'll break his heart. And I won't have that, am I making myself clear?"

"Yes, Mom."

She got up. "Now, get in the shower and start getting ready. We're not going to be late. I don't want him looking up in the stands and not seeing us there." The door shut behind her.

Eric sighed. He glanced at a framed picture on his wall. There was a large team photo, with a sign in front of the seated guys on the front row: Woodbridge Wildcats State Champions. In the lower right-hand corner of the frame was a circular mounted individual portrait. He was wearing his baseball uniform and was kneeling on one knee. In one hand he was holding a baseball bat, in the other a glove. He looked closer at the picture. He was standing in the back row. On his left was Chris, on his right was Sean.

He frowned. *Sean was an athlete?*

He walked back over to the desk and picked up his yearbook again. He found Sean's name in the yearbook. There were only the two photos of him listed—so he wasn't on any sports teams at Woodbridge High.

He swallowed. *Did he give up sports because of me?*

His phone chirped again.

He stared at it, almost afraid to look at it.

He took a deep breath and picked it up.

The text was from Chris: *are we cool, man?*

He smiled, and typed back: *yeah, we're cool. No worries.*

He walked into the bathroom and turned on the shower.

Going to the game might be a good idea, he thought as he undressed. *Maybe it'll get my mind off things. And it's not a bad idea to be seen in public—let people know I don't care what they say or think.*

He started whistling as he got into the shower.

CHAPTER FOURTEEN

The parking lot by the high school baseball field was full. Mom had to drive around before she finally found a space. She smiled. "Looks like everyone in town is here."

It was just after seven and the sun was setting over the mountains in the west. The lights on the field were on. "I hope Danny doesn't notice we're late," Mom said as she unbuckled her seat belt with one hand while she turned off the engine with the other.

Just one more thing he'll blame me for, Eric thought as he removed his own seat belt and opened the car door. *Maybe being here will trigger another memory*, he thought as Mom clicked the button to lock the car. It chirped and the headlights flashed, and she dropped her keys into her purse.

She handed him a twenty. "Look, I know you don't want to be here," she said in a quiet voice as they walked across the parking lot, "but I'm not going to embarrass you by making you sit with me. You can go sit with your friends. Just make sure you find your father and me when the game's over, so one of us can drive you home. Understood?"

He slid the twenty into his shorts pocket and smiled at her. "Thanks, Mom." Inwardly, he sighed. *I should have called Lacey or Chris and asked them to meet me here*, he thought. *I'm not going to recognize anyone else.* Aloud, he said, "I'm going to get a Coke. You go ahead and find a seat."

"All right." She kissed him on the cheek. "Remember to find us—don't make me come looking for you. If I have to, I *will* embarrass you."

He watched her walk away toward the bleachers, and took a deep breath. The concession stand was set up about thirty yards away from the field, and he started walking across the grass. There was a short line—some adults, some kids—and he got in line behind them. He pulled his phone out of his pocket and texted Lacey: *what are you doing? I'm at Danny's baseball game.*

He was about to send a text to Chris when someone said his name. He turned. "Yes?"

It was a tall, slender boy about his own age. His hair was dirty blond and parted in the middle. Braces gleamed on his teeth. He was wearing a baggy shirt over a long pair of baggy basketball shorts hanging just past his knees. His face was dotted with pimples. He was grinning. "Hey, man, don't you remember me?" The two shorter boys with him started laughing. "Oh, yeah." He put his hand up to his mouth. "You have *amnesia*, don't you?"

Eric felt his cheeks start to burn. He nodded and forced a smile on his face. "Sorry, yeah." He started to turn back around but the kid grabbed his arm. He pulled free. "What's your problem?" he asked.

The blond kid stuck his face right into his, and Eric could smell his breath. "*You're* my problem," he jeered as the other two boys laughed again. The boy pushed Eric in the chest, and Eric stumbled back a bit into the person in line in front of him.

"Sorry," Eric muttered. He gritted his teeth. "Don't ever touch me again."

"What are you going to do?" The blond kid pushed him again.

Eric punched him square in the nose, and felt the cartilage give beneath his fist. Blood started spurting out of the kid's nose as he staggered back.

Blood.

There's so much blood. It's everywhere.

He felt dizzy, and there was a roaring in his ears.

"You said you wanted to help me," Sean said. His blue eyes were filled with tears. "Did you mean it, Eric?"

"Of course I meant it. I owe you that much. You can't keep dealing drugs, Sean. You're going to get caught and your life is going to be ruined."

Sean turned his back and walked a few steps away. His shoulders hunched down. "Are you going to rat me out to your uncle?"

"Of course not."

"You don't understand." Sean turned back around. Tears were rolling down his cheeks. "You couldn't possibly understand."

"Then tell me, Sean. Make me understand."

His lower lip quivered. "This wasn't my idea, Eric. You think I want to do this? I don't have a choice. I have to."

"You always have a choice, Sean."

Sean bit his lower lip. "I've hated you for years, you know that? I've absolutely hated you, I wished you were dead so many times I can't even count them." He shook his head. "But now that you're here—I don't know. I don't know that I can go through with it."

"What—what are you talking about?"

"Get out of here," Sean said in a low voice. "Get in your car and drive and don't look back."

"Sean—"

"I'm serious." Sean grabbed his arm. *"You have to get out of here before it's too late."*

"I don't understand, you asked me to come—"

"Son, are you all right?"

Eric shook his head, and was back at the baseball field. The blond kid was standing with a bloody napkin pressed to his nose, a security guard holding his other arm. His friends were nowhere to be seen. He looked at the man standing next to him. He was also in a security guard's uniform. "That was a hell of a punch." The guard grinned at him. "You may have broken his nose."

"I'm—I'm fine." Eric replied. He shook his head again. "Who is that kid?"

"Bill Shaughnessy," a girl said from just behind him. "He's a thug. He deserves worse."

Eric turned his head. She'd visited him in the hospital— *Connie Hansen*, he remembered. She smiled at him. "How are you, Eric?"

Warmth began to spread through his body again, and he was aware of a tingling in his fingertips. He nodded. "I've been better but I think I'm okay now."

"We can call the police, if you'd like," the security guard went on. "Or throw him out of here."

"I don't want him arrested."

The guard walked over to his colleague, but before they could do anything, Eric asked Bill, "Why did you want to fight me?"

"You and your stupid friends think you're better than everyone else," he spat, "then you kill someone and you get away with it because your uncle's the sheriff. You make me sick."

"I didn't kill anyone."

"Yeah, right."

"Come on, you little punk," the guard holding him said, and dragged him away.

The other guard whistled. "That one's a nasty piece of work. He'll wind up in jail one day, mark my words." He patted Eric on the shoulder. "Forget what he said. Just go on up and enjoy the game, son, he won't be bothering you again tonight." He tipped his hat and walked away.

A bat cracked and the crowd cheered.

"How are you *really*?" Connie asked once the guard was out of earshot. She tucked her arm through his. "Come on, let's walk over to the bleachers. We can talk on the way," she said. They started walking. "Why don't you come sit with us?" She beamed at him. "It'll be like old times. The whole gang's here. Jemal. Bobby, Tessa—everyone will be so glad to see you."

He froze when she mentioned the names. *Jemal, Bobby— they were there that night in Oakhurst, the night Paul Benson...* He gulped. "Actually, Lacey's meeting me here," he replied. "We're—we're trying to get things worked out..."

"Say no more!" Connie bumped him with her shoulder. "But come find us if you change your mind, okay? It really is good to see you."

He watched her walk away, biting his lip.

"Eric!"

It was Lacey.

She was wearing a pair of khaki shorts and a pale blue shirt with UCLA written in gold script across her chest. Her hair was loose and bouncing as she walked quickly through the grass.

Lacey squeezed his arm. "Who was that you were talking to? I couldn't tell—it's too dark. Why are you hanging out here in the shadows, anyway?"

Eric turned, but Connie had made it to the bleachers and disappeared.

Eric grinned back at her. "It was Connie, and no, you have no reason to be jealous."

Lacey hooked her arm through his. "What did she want?"

"It doesn't matter." They started walking. There was another cheer from the crowd. He looked up at the scoreboard. The visiting team was up 2–0 in the third inning. "Thanks for coming. Mom doesn't want me to be home alone, so she made me come—but I don't know anyone here. I'm glad you came."

"I'm glad you asked me." She put her head against his arm as they reached the steps up to the bleachers. They climbed up to the very top row and sat down. He could see his parents sitting farther down—his mother looked up and waved, a big smile on her face. He smiled back at her, enjoying the feel of Lacey's leg pressed up against his, the warmth radiating from her arm tucked through his.

It felt right.

Danny was playing right field, and got a base hit in the fourth inning. The crowd cheered, and Eric felt himself relaxing. The score was now tied, 2–2.

But then the Woodbridge team came in, and their coach came out of the dugout to talk to the pitcher.

It was Coach Walton.

Eric stiffened.

Coach Walton turned and looked up into the stands, still talking to the pitcher.

Eric shrank in his seat.

"Eric?" Lacey asked. "Are you okay?"

And then Coach Walton handed the baseball over, pressing it into the pitcher's hand.

I can't believe I forgot my stupid keys, raced through his mind as he pushed the locker room door open and walked inside. I haven't been thinking clearly since I broke up with Lacey. He stopped walking and leaned against the wall. The pain was so visceral. How could she do that to me? I thought she loved me! And with Chris, of all people. He felt tears coming again. "Man up," he told himself again, angrily wiping at his eyes. He walked around the corner into the locker room when he heard voices.

"You got the money?"

"Uh-huh."

"You're doing great, kid."

It was Coach Walton's voice. Curious, he could see the light on in Coach Walton's office.

The "kid" was Sean Brody.

Sean was handing Coach Walton a wad of cash.

What the hell?

He pulled his phone out of his pocket and clicked the camera icon. He held the phone up to his face just as Coach Walton handed a baggie full of pills to Sean. He clicked quickly, taking three clear pictures.

He turned and ran out of the locker room.

Coach Walton.

His breathing started coming heavily.

"Eric? Are you okay?" Lacey's voice sounded a million miles away.

How am I going to get home without my keys? I guess I'll have to wait for them to leave and then go back. The parking lot was hot—the sun was really bright. Coach Walton's truck was parked underneath a tree in the shade. Coach Walton is a drug dealer.

Uncle Arnie's voice from dinner the other night: "We're

developing a serious problem with drugs over at the college campus. There's ecstasy everywhere—one kid almost died from it last weekend. I don't know where it's coming from, but we've got to find the source before someone dies."

Coach Walton was the source.

Sean Brody was dealing it for him.

I have to tell Uncle Arnie.

But Coach Walton has a wife and a daughter. What'll happen to them if he goes to jail?

But if I don't do anything some kid I don't even know might die.

And Sean—what about Sean? We used to be friends, until he made that pass at Chris on the campout.

I've got to hide somewhere until they leave.

Ah, the bushes. I'll just duck down behind the bushes until they're gone, then I'll get my keys and figure out what I'm going to do.

"Eric? Are you okay? Please answer me."

"Sorry." He gave Lacey a weak smile. "Sorry."

"You scared me." She playfully pinched his arm. "Don't do that again."

"You can come out now, Eric," Sean called.

"How did you know—"

"I saw you in the locker room and your car is right there. Don't worry, Coach didn't see you. I knew you were hiding out here somewhere waiting for us to leave."

"Are you crazy? What the hell do you think you're doing, Sean?"

"What do you care? Are you going to go to your uncle? You took pictures of us, didn't you?"

"Yes, I did. Why didn't you say something to Coach?"

"Because we used to be friends. Because you used to be a

nice guy. I don't know what Coach would do. He's a dangerous man, Eric."

"Why are you doing it, Sean? I—I can't believe you would deal drugs."

"You can't?" Sean smirked at him. "You never had a problem believing the worst of me before."

"Look, I'm sorry. Tell me. Why? Why are you doing this?"

"I can't tell you. I wish I could but I can't."

"You have to stop, Sean."

"Why do you care? Don't you hate me?"

"I never hated you."

"You could have fooled me." He laughed. "Man, if you don't hate me, I sure don't want to see how you'd treat someone you do hate. You've made my life a living hell for the last three years."

"Look, I was wrong, okay?"

"And that's supposed to make up for making my life hell? For turning your back on me like I was a disease or something? We used to be friends, Eric. We used to be like brothers."

"Sean—"

He climbed on his bike. "Do what you want to, Eric, like you always do. I don't give a shit anymore." He rode off.

The Woodbridge team was running in off the field. It was the bottom of the sixth inning, and the score was still 2–2. The crowd was cheering.

Eric swallowed.

Coach Walton was pacing in front of the dugout. When Danny made it in, he put his arm around Danny's shoulders and looked back up into the bleachers as he talked to him.

Their eyes met. Coach Walton smirked at Eric.

"Get away from him, Danny," Eric said to himself. He reached for his cell phone and scrolled through the contacts.

His uncle wasn't listed.

"I haven't gone to my uncle because I don't want you to get in trouble."

"Like you care." Sean's bike was leaning against a tree where the clearing of the Ledge ended in an incline.

"Sean, I do care. I do. I know I've been an asshole. It was just—such a shock to know about you, what you tried to do with Chris and—"

"You're such an idiot." Sean shook his head. *"You have no clue. I didn't make a pass at Chris—Chris made a pass at ME. He was into it, Eric, right up until the minute you woke up and he got scared. He was into it then, and he's been into it ever since."*

"But…but…but that doesn't make any sense."

"Chris LOVES me, Eric. We're both going to UC–Santa Barbara next year so we can finally be together. Far away from this horrible little hick town. I don't care if I ever come back here."

"That's—that's great."

Sean stared at him. *"What do you mean?"*

"It's great. I've done a lot of thinking since the whole Lacey thing happened. I was wrong for what I did to you, Sean. We WERE friends. I cared about you. I shouldn't have turned my back on you the way I did. It was wrong. I should have been supportive. It didn't change who you were. You're still you. I am so sorry. About everything. But you've got to stop dealing the drugs, Sean. You and Chris can't ever have a future if you get busted. I'm not going to turn you and Coach in—but someone else will. And your life is going to be ruined."

Sean just blinked at him. *"You need to get out of here,"* he said after a few moments of silence. He looked past Eric into the woods. *"Seriously, man, get in your car and get the hell out of here."*

"I'm not going anywhere—"

"I don't want you to die." Sean's face was panicked. "I never did, I'm so sorry, but you've got to get out of here. It's almost too late."

"What are you talking about?"

"There isn't time to explain! GO!"

Sean shoved him just as Eric heard the crack of a gunshot. Sean's eyes widened and his hands flew to his midsection. Blood spurted out between his fingers.

He gurgled and went down.

"You have...to get...out of here," Sean wheezed, his face a mask of shock and pain. "He's...going to...kill you...he made me...lure you...out here...he made me...do everything...he threatened...he threatened...to expose me and Chris...Chris... couldn't...handle it...I protected him..."

"I can't leave you here. Come on, let's get you into my car."

Sean didn't feel heavy. Blood was everywhere.

So much blood.

The engine started.

"I'm...so...sorry, Eric. Tell Chris...I love him..."

"Stop that, we're going to get you to a hospital and everything's going to be okay, so just hold on, okay, Sean?"

Dust flew as the car spun out and as it came around, Coach Walton was up in a tree, holding a gun—

"Lacey, do you know my uncle's phone number, by any chance?"

But as he spoke the batter swung and connected. The crowd leaped to its feet cheering as he took off for first base. The ball flew through the air heading for the back fence as the crowd cheered.

I'm going too fast I need to slow down but he doesn't

look good oh God there's so much blood Sean I'm so sorry for
everything, I'll get you to the hospital.

The ball landed behind the fence as the crowd cheered. The
batter was rounding the bases.

Eric felt sick.

The evidence was in my phone, and my phone is gone.

But I remember now.

I've got to call Uncle Arnie.

MOM has his number.

The team was out on the field, dogpiling the batter.

Coach Walton was standing in front of the dug out, smiling.
He was looking up into the crowd.

Eric fumbled his phone out.

The crowd was pouring out of the bleachers and running out
onto the field. Lacey was still standing, yelling.

He saw Coach Walton put his arm around Danny's shoulders
again.

"No," he whispered, dialing 911.

"Nine-one-one, what's your emergency?"

Danny was getting into Coach Walton's truck.

Eric stood up, forgetting the phone call. "NO DANNY NO!"
he screamed at the top of his lungs.

He started running down the bleachers.

He heard Lacey calling his name, but he ignored her. He
darted around people, shoved past others, ignoring the dirty looks
he was getting. There was a logjam of people on the ramp, so he
climbed over the railing and dropped three feet to the ground. He
almost lost his balance, but managed to get his footing again and
started running.

The truck's lights came on.

His breathing was becoming more labored. He got a stitch in
his side but he ignored it. His injured ankle started complaining

but he kept running. When he was halfway to the parking lot, the blue truck backed out of its spot, shifted gears, and sped out of the lot. Its tires squealed as it turned onto the street.

Eric stopped running, tears of anger and frustration rising in his eyes. He tried to catch his breath, and finally bent over at the waist and put his head down.

What is he doing with Danny?

"Eric, what the hell was that all about?" Lacey jogged up to him, her face angry.

"Coach—and Danny—" he gasped out, still not able to get his breathing under control.

"Here." She handed him the bottle of water she was carrying. Gratefully he took it drained it. "Now, will you tell me what's going on?"

"Coach, it's Coach," he finally managed to get out. He was still holding his phone, but the 911 operator had long since hung up. "Coach killed Sean."

Her eyes widened. "Eric, you can't mean that." She stared at him, her mouth open.

He grabbed her. "I *remember*, Lacey. I remember everything." He gripped her tightly. "Your birthday is September fourteenth. Your cat's name is Darcy, after *Pride and Prejudice* because that's your favorite book. You want to go to Berkeley and major in political science, and maybe be a lawyer. I first asked you out when we were freshmen at the victory dance after the first football game, when we beat Sonora for the first time in ten years. I *remember*." He let go of her, wincing when he saw the red marks where his fingers had dug into her skin. "It was Coach, Lacey. He killed Sean—but it wasn't Sean he was trying to kill. It was *me*."

"Oh my God." Her face went white. "And Danny's with him?" she half whispered. "What are we going to do?"

Before he could answer, his phone rang. He stared at it for a second.

Danny's face was smiling at him from the screen, and across the top it read *Danny Calling*.

He answered. "Danny?"

"Eric?" Danny's voice sounded frightened, like he was on the verge of tears. "Eric, I have a message for you from Coach Walton." In the background Eric could hear other cars.

"Okay, Danny. Go ahead."

"He wants you to come to the Ledge, and don't tell anyone." His voice choked for a moment. "Come alone. You can't tell anyone. Not Mom, not Dad, no one. Not the police. If you don't"—he caught his breath again—"if you don't come by yourself, he said he's going to kill me."

"Danny—"

The call disconnected.

Eric stared at the phone in horror.

"What did he say?" Lacey asked.

"Give me your car keys." Eric ran his fingers through his hair. *Oh God, oh God. He's going to kill Danny.* "I have to go out to the Ledge or he's going to kill Danny."

"Oh my God." Lacey dug her keys out of her purse with shaking hands. "What do you want me to do?"

"Call my uncle and tell him everything." Eric's own hands were shaking so hard he almost dropped the keys. "And find my parents."

She nodded. "Please, Eric. Be careful. Please." She leaned up and kissed him on the cheek.

He turned and ran to the parking lot.

Chapter Fifteen

He was driving too fast and knew he should slow down. He wasn't used to driving Lacey's car, didn't know how it handled. But he couldn't. He had to risk it. *Danny's in danger and it's my fault. If anything happens to him...* He forced that thought out of his mind. He couldn't allow himself to think that way. He had to stay positive and focused on the problem at hand. Freaking out wouldn't do Danny any good.

He weaved around cars, ran yellow lights as they turned red, and hoped against hope he wouldn't get pulled over. There wasn't time to explain to a patrol cop. With every passing second, the feeling he might not ever see Danny alive again grew stronger. "Get out of my way!" he screamed at a yellow Taurus going maybe fifteen miles per hour. He eased his foot over to the brake. There were no cars coming from the opposite direction so he swung the car to the left and went around the Taurus, angrily pressing the palm of his hand down on the horn.

His phone vibrated in his pocket, but he didn't bother getting it. He couldn't take his eyes off the road, couldn't be distracted from anything but getting to the Ledge as fast as he possibly could. He didn't know what he'd do when he got there—he had no idea. But maybe Coach would let Danny go.

He gripped the steering wheel tighter. He just prayed Lacey was able to reach his uncle—or his mother was able to.

Memories of his brother kept flashing through his mind, and he tried shutting them off. But now that he'd broken through the amnesia, he couldn't seem to stop memories from crowding into his mind. He tried to focus on breathing deeply—long, slow inhales and exhales. His heart was pounding so hard it felt like it was hitting his ribs.

He remembered everything now, and each memory simply triggered more memories.

I'm a terrible brother kept repeating after every memory of every name he'd ever called Danny, every awful thing he'd ever done to him—the time he broke Danny's nose, the time he'd left him at the mall. *No wonder he hates me.* He remembered ignoring him in the cafeteria at the high school, not stopping some of his teammates on the football team from hazing him, and laughing with them as they pantsed him in the locker room and pushed him out into the hallway in just his underwear.

He shook his head. *I hope I get the chance to say I'm sorry and make it up to him.*

Don't think like that. There's no reason for Coach Walton to hurt him.

"It's me he wants," he said out loud.

It was all too clear now. Taking the picture with his phone, not knowing what to do with it, horrified by the reality his coach—a well-respected figure in town—was the drug source his uncle was looking for. It was just another horrible blow, and he hadn't known what to do.

In that last week before the accident his entire world had collapsed. The guilt of contributing to Paul Benson's suicide—of being the straw that broke his back and pushed him over the edge.

Lacey and Chris—tears filled his eyes as the pain came back. He'd been like a zombie, wandering around not knowing what to do, wondering what he'd ever done to deserve such a horrible betrayal by the two people he cared about the most.

Knowing he'd done something worse to Sean, someone who'd been like a brother to him for almost his entire life—that he could have pushed Sean over the edge like Paul Benson.

The conflict of not knowing what to do, knowing he had to turn the picture over to Uncle Arnie but not wanting to ruin Sean's life more than he already had.

The terrible knowledge he'd never really known his best friend, not really, because Chris had never felt like he could be honest with him.

And Coach Walton—who'd have ever believed he was a drug dealer? He was a hero around town, the man who'd rescued the football team from being a perennial loser and turned it into an annual state championship contender. Eric had never been close to Coach, but he hadn't disliked him either.

His head had felt like it was going to explode.

So, of course when he got the message from Sean on Facebook, he'd agreed to go to the Ledge. He'd hoped to convince Sean to stop dealing the drugs, come up with some kind of plan to get him out from under Coach's thumb.

He'd been full of hope that morning as he drove out there. Once he and Sean had everything figured out, he'd talk to Chris and get everything straightened out with him. He'd go see Lacey and try to put the broken pieces of their relationship back together.

Only to see Sean get shot down right in front of him.

There was so much blood.

He passed the last of the streetlights as he reached the edge of town and pressed down on the accelerator. The speedometer needle jumped from fifty to seventy and kept climbing.

There was no moon, and as soon as he left the city limits he was plunged into what seemed like absolute darkness. The sky was a velvety dark navy blue. The headlights of Lacey's car cut through the darkness, but outside the cones of light was pure black. It was eerie. He just hoped a deer wouldn't jump out of the woods in front of the car.

The car was out of control, he couldn't keep it from spinning out of the curve. The guardrail was getting closer. Everything was moving in slow motion, it didn't seem real, this couldn't be happening. Then the car plunged through the guardrail and flew into the air. He screamed as he saw blue sky for what seemed like an eternity, but the front end of his car dipped down as gravity grabbed hold and now the ground was rushing up and his air bag exploded open. The front end of the car hit the ground with a jarring crash as windows shattered and he heard Sean hit the back of the front seat with a terrible thump and the car flipped over and kept flipping over until it finally came to rest. He could hear the engine ticking, and steam was rising from under the front hood. He could smell the chemicals as the air bag deflated, and as it went down he saw that the windshield was gone except for jagged pieces here and there spiderwebbed with cracks. Everything hurt and he could barely breathe, but he somehow managed to twist around—his neck screaming in agony as he did—to check on Sean. Sean gurgled, and a bubble of blood passed through his lips, but he was smiling.

And then everything went black.

He shook his head, blinking back tears. *You have to stay calm and focused*, he reminded himself. *Danny's life depends on it.*

He eased up a little on the gas pedal, gulping in air.

The curve where he'd crashed was coming up.

Lacey's car protested but took the curve, centrifugal force making his side of the car rise. For a second it seemed the car might go up on just the two right wheels. But it held and the car righted itself.

He blew out a sigh of relief and pushed down on the accelerator again.

I never imagined Sean was killed by mistake, no one did, he thought as he came out of the curve. There was no one else on the road, and he hoped Lacey was able to track down his uncle.

But it might be too late by the time they get here.

Don't think that way! As long as Danny is still alive…he's still alive!

He gulped again. *Everything's going to be okay, just keep thinking that, Coach doesn't want to hurt Danny, he doesn't want Danny, he wants me and he's getting what he wants. Just hang in there, Danny, and don't make him mad, don't do anything stupid. I'm coming, and I'm so sorry about everything. You deserved a better brother than me.*

The headlights caught the entrance to the Ledge and he slowed down.

And he remembered.

Why does Sean want me to meet him out here?

He waited for a white Malibu to pass in the opposite direction, and took the turn slowly. I'll destroy the picture in front of him, let him know that his secret is safe with me, but I'll talk him out of dealing, I've got to get him to stop. We can be friends again and I can make up for everything I've done.

The car came out into the clearing, and Sean was standing at the very edge. He turned and looked, a big smile on his face.

He turned and started down the slope, his foot on the brake.

And when he reached the Ledge, his headlights illuminated the blue truck parked near the tree line to the left.

He stopped the car but didn't turn off the headlights. He shut off the engine and got out of the car. "Danny?" he yelled.

"Turn off the lights," Coach Walton ordered from behind him. "You didn't call your uncle, did you? I'd hate to have to hurt Danny." His tone was mocking. "He's such a good kid."

Eric reached inside the car and flicked the lights off. "Where's Danny?" he asked, turning to face the direction Coach's voice was coming from. "Is he okay? You haven't hurt him, have you?"

"Your brother is fine—for now. I have a gun to his head, and he knows only to talk when I tell him to. But how he is in a few minutes, well, I guess that all depends on you."

"You're not going to get away with this. People saw Danny get into your truck. How *did* you get him to go with you?"

"I told him I had proof you killed Sean Brody." Eric could hear the smugness in Coach Walton's voice. "And I'd give it to him right after the game. When Kirk hit that home run to win it, it was our chance. Nobody saw us leave—they were too busy celebrating."

"Lacey did. She gave me the keys to her car so I could get out here. It's over, Coach. Let him go."

"She'll be too distraught to think clearly when she gets the news about her loverboy's sad suicide." Coach Walton laughed. "When she realizes you borrowed her car just so you could come out to where you killed Sean so you could take your own life in remorse, she'll be crushed. She might even decide to join you."

The implied threat wasn't lost on Eric. He swallowed. He tried to keep his voice level. "You're not thinking clearly, Coach."

Despite his best efforts, his voice still shook. "I didn't kill Sean, and my uncle already knows. I told him."

"Half the town thinks your uncle is letting you get away with it already," Coach taunted. "After they find your body, no one will believe anything he says."

"So, you're just going to shoot me? How could you make that look like a suicide?"

"You're going to send your girlfriend a suicide text," Coach Walton went on like Eric hadn't said anything. "You're going to tell her you remember killing Sean, and you can't live with yourself anymore."

"She knows I came out here because Danny was with you."

"Danny asked me for a ride because he was worried about you. You sent him a suicide text and we raced out here as quick as we could. We tried to save you—but we didn't get here in time. We got here just in time to see you jump off the side."

It might work. "Danny will never go along with that," Eric replied, praying it was true. *I can't blame him if does.*

"Won't he? He really hates you, you know." The voice from the darkness mocked him. Eric tried to peer through the darkness but couldn't see anything. "You weren't much of a brother, you know. He's told me all about you, Eric. I wouldn't treat a dog the way you treat him."

"I'm still his brother." Eric bit his lip. "Brothers get mad at each other, that's normal."

"Then maybe you shot and killed Danny, shot me, and then jumped. Of course, you didn't kill me. Yes, that could work. It would be painful, but I can handle it." He heard movement, and he again tried to see through the darkness. "Yes, I like the sound of that. Thanks, Eric—that's an even better plan."

He's lost his mind, we're out here with a crazy man with a gun. Come on, Uncle Arnie! Where are you? "Where is Danny?" *Think, Eric, think! Do something!*

"Danny's here, with me, like I said. I told you, he's only going to speak when I let him."

"How do I know you haven't already killed him?" Eric asked. "I want to hear him say something. Danny!"

"Go ahead, Danny, say hello to your rotten big brother."

He heard some movement in the darkness—and saw vague shapes. He squinted but couldn't get a good look. Danny yelled, "Eric, get in the car and go!"

"I can't leave you here." Eric struggled to keep his voice steady.

I can't leave you here to die.

God needs you to be strong, Karly's voice echoed in his mind.

"Let him go, Coach, and I'll do whatever you want," Eric pleaded. "I'm begging you. I'll do whatever you want as long as you let him go."

You were meant to die in that accident, but God saved you for a greater purpose.

With a rush of clarity, it all made sense to him.

I was supposed to die in the accident, but God let me live so I could save Danny's life.

Maybe God DID speak to Karly.

And as soon as he thought it, images started flooding through his mind.

He saw Danny, with a big smile on his face, crossing the stage at school and accepting his diploma. Danny, in a crowd of students on a football field he knew instantly as USC's, in a cap and gown, graduating from college. Danny, in scrubs in an emergency room, resuscitating a patient.

And Danny standing at the side of a grave, tears flowing

down his face. "I can never, ever thank you enough, Eric. You died saving my life. I'm so sorry, so terribly sorry, for all the horrible things I thought about you, all the things I said to you that last week before you died. I'll spend the rest of my life making up for it. I hope you know how much I love you, how much I miss you, that I would give anything to have you here with me now. I love you, Eric. I'm so sorry."

Tears pricked at the corners of Eric's eyes. He steeled his courage and stood up straight. And when he spoke again, his voice was steady and strong. "If you let him go, Coach, I'll jump. I'll send the text to Lacey. I'll confess to killing Sean. Just let him go, Coach, and it all ends here."

You were a sleeping angel, Eric, with the capacity to do great good. You just didn't realize it.

"Please, Coach." Eric reached into his pocket and pulled out his cell phone. "I'll text her right now." He hit the activate button, and the screen glowed in the dark. There was a message on the screen: *Talked to your uncle. He said not to do anything crazy and he's on his way.*

"Toss me the phone," Coach commanded.

Eric erased the message. "Don't you want me to text Lacey and—"

"I'm not stupid," Coach replied. "I'll send the damned message! Now toss me the damned phone!"

"I don't know where to toss it." *Throw it over the Ledge! No, he'll kill Danny if you do that. But you can't let him have your phone!*

He clearly heard the sound of the gun being cocked. "Throw me the phone or I'll shoot him right now."

"Don't do it!" Danny shouted. "Get in the car and get out of here, Eric!"

"Aw, isn't that sweet?" Coach mocked. "The two brothers,

trying to save each other. I'm almost touched. Too little, too late, boys! Hey, Eric, did you know that Danny was the one who told me you were out walking in the woods the other night? So I could get a shot at you? He didn't care so much about keeping you alive then, did you, Danny?"

"I didn't know he was going to try to shoot you!" Danny shouted. "He said he just wanted to talk to you!"

"It's okay, Danny." Eric took a deep breath and closed his eyes. "I know you wouldn't have done it if you knew."

"THROW ME THE GODDAMNED PHONE!"

Eric tossed the phone in the direction of their voices. The still-lit screen glowed as the phone turned over and over in the air, casting a small circle of light as it went. For a brief second, he saw Danny's face before the phone dropped to the ground, still glowing.

"Pick it up, Danny, and hand it to me."

Eric took a careful step toward where he'd seen Danny. When nothing was said, he took another. The glow floated up from the ground, illuminating Danny's arm, and he took a few more steps as Danny handed the phone to Coach. For a brief second, he caught a glimpse of Coach Walton.

And the gun he was holding in his other hand.

The glow disappeared.

Praying he didn't step on something that would make a noise, Eric held his breath as he took another couple of steps forward. He was about to take another when a flashlight shone in his face, blinding him. He put a hand up over his eyes.

"Stay where you are." There was a thud, Danny cried out briefly, then the sound of a body hitting the ground.

"Danny?"

Coach laughed and the sound sent chills up Eric's spine. "Don't worry about him. I just gave him a little tap on the head so I could deal with you. By the time he comes to, it'll be all over. Maybe I'll just shoot him while he's out, so he just never wakes up. Now turn around."

Eric turned around and felt the nose of the gun shoved into his back.

"Start walking."

Eric took a step forward. *Where's Uncle Arnie? What's taking him so long?* "So, why did you start dealing drugs, Coach?"

"Shut up and walk."

"It must have been a shock when you shot Sean instead of me." Eric took a few more steps.

"Yeah, it was." Coach shoved the gun harder against his back. "I didn't react right away. By the time I realized what happened, you had him in your car and were driving away. I thought for sure my goose was cooked. I got in my truck and followed, but you had quite a head start—and then I heard the crash. Lucky for me you're a shitty driver, too. I pulled over on the side of the road, and there was your car, smashed up down the gully. I climbed down and there you were. Sean was dead, so I took his phone. You barely had a pulse, so I took your phone too, and figured by the time someone got out there, you'd be dead."

"Must have quite a shock when you found out I was alive." *I've got to keep him talking*, Eric thought, listening for the sound of sirens in the distance.

He didn't hear any.

"Yeah, well," Coach responded. He barked out another laugh. "But you were in a coma, so that bought me some time. But then you woke up—with amnesia."

"What a lucky break for you."

"For me?" He laughed again. "It was a lucky break for *you*. As long as you couldn't remember anything, I was safe—and pretty much everyone in town thought you'd killed Sean. I was pretty certain even if you did remember, I could deny everything. It was your word against mine—and I'd destroyed your phone."

Eric felt sick to his stomach.

"I'd started winning over your brother—it was pathetic how easy that was. You really are a rotten brother—and your parents aren't much better. He was so desperate for anyone to pay attention to him, it was a piece of cake. He kept me informed on everything—and I told him I wanted to talk to you privately, so I could see for myself how you were doing and if you'd be able to play football this fall. So, when you went out into the woods, he texted me right away."

Eric closed his eyes. "Of course. You live right down the street from us."

"Alas, you moved right after I fired." Coach shook his head. "I suppose that would have been too easy, a shooting accident in the woods. But it almost worked. And you didn't have any idea how close you came to death."

Eric could hear the stream in the little valley below the Ledge much more clearly now. He took another tentative step forward, and his heel came down on the edge, his toes in the air. He stopped walking.

"Move it!" Coach prodded him with the gun again.

"We're at the edge, Coach." He turned around as Coach flicked the flashlight off. "So, I guess this is good-bye, huh?"

"You probably won't believe this, but I'm sorry it came to this, Eric." There was a note of regret in his voice. "I never wanted to kill anyone, you know. You never should have taken that picture. If you hadn't, Sean would still be alive and everything would be just fine. Now, go on and step off the edge."

Eric took a deep breath, and turned around.

He moved his right hand and knocked the gun away. It went

off, deafening him, and he moved to one side, hoping against hope the edge didn't curve away in that direction, and kicked at Coach's legs.

"Damn you!" Coach screamed and shoved against Eric's chest.

Eric lost his balance and grabbed on to Coach's hands.

And he went over backward.

As he went, he held Coach's arms with a death grip.

"Nooooooo!" Coach screamed.

It seemed liked they floated forever through the air.

But then he hit the side of the incline with his back and all of his breath rushed out of him. He let go of Coach's arms, and he started sliding. He reached out his hands, clawing at the ground, desperately trying to grab something, anything, to stop him from falling.

And he hit a bush, grasped it with both hands, and stopped moving.

Breathing hard, he closed his eyes. Below he could hear the rushing water.

And a flashlight shone directly in his face.

He'd only fallen about eight feet.

He heard the gun cock again.

"Eric?" he heard Danny's voice ask. "Where's Coach?"

"I...don't...know...My...ribs..." He was having trouble breathing. "We...both...went...over..."

The beam of the flashlight scanned the incline.

"I don't see him anywhere," Danny called down. "Are you okay?"

Relief flooded through him. "My...ribs...might...have... broken...some."

"Well, hold on! I'll see if I can find something in the car to pull you up with."

The light went away, plunging the side of the cliff into darkness again.

And in the distance, he finally heard the welcome sound of a police siren.

He closed his eyes.

EPILOGUE

A few days later

"Are you sure you want to do this by yourself?" Lacey asked, turning the car off and looking over at him. "We don't mind going with you."

Eric smiled back at her. "I appreciate that, but I kind of need to do this by myself. But I'm glad you both came with me."

"No problem, bro." Chris said from the backseat, clapping one of his hands on Eric's left shoulder.

Eric opened the car door and got out. Chris handed him the dozen red roses. "You sure?" Chris asked again, as Eric took the roses and cradled them in his arms.

He smiled back at Chris. "Yeah, I'm sure," he replied. "I just have to go slow, is all." Chris gave him another grin and got back into the car.

Eric carefully made his way through the cemetery. He'd broken two ribs, and there were several bands of tape around his chest. Sometimes if he moved too fast, he got out of breath and the pain came back, but he found if he took his time he was fine.

Coach Walton's body had been found about a mile downstream, snagged on a fallen tree. His neck had snapped when he hit the water. In the basement of his house they'd found the lab where he made the ecstasy. His wife, it turned out, had majored in chemistry in college. She'd been arrested—her parents came up from Fresno to take their two-year-old daughter.

Eric felt sorry for her. She was claiming he was abusive and beat her, forced her to make the drugs. Given that he was also a murderer, it wasn't too much of a stretch to believe her story.

It was a beautiful day. A few clouds drifted across the blue sky, and there was a nice breeze blowing. He'd never been in the cemetery before—he knew some of the kids from the high school liked to party in there sometimes, but he'd never been one of them—and he was amazed at how peaceful and quiet it was.

The truth about Chris and Sean had also come out. Chris had been right—his father had completely lost it and thrown him out, disowning him. He was staying in the spare bedroom of the Matthews house, for as long as he needed to. Eric was proud of Chris. It couldn't have been easy, but he refused to allow people to think Sean had been a drug dealer without knowing why he did it. "It's not fair to Sean," Chris said. "He was too good a person."

He really was, Eric thought as he found his grave. There was just a simple granite marker, with his name and the dates of his life. To the right of his grave was a marker for his father. His eyes filled with tears. *I'm so sorry for everything, Sean*, he thought as he knelt down to place the roses beneath the marker. *I'm sorry I was so stupid. You were a great guy and because I was an idiot—* He choked up a bit. *I just wish I could have saved you. At the end, though, you knew, you knew I was sorry and trying to make amends.*

He looked back in the direction of the car. Lacey was sitting on the hood.

Somehow, after everything that happened, her mistake didn't seem quite so serious anymore. *It's not like I have to be jealous of Chris anyway*. He smiled. They were taking things slow, but if the past few days were any indication, things were going to be just fine, if not better than before.

I've changed, too, he thought as he looked down at Sean's marker. *I'll never again be the shallow boy who doesn't care how his behavior hurts other people.*

"Your mother told me I'd find you here."

Eric looked across the grave at Christian Karly and gave her a gentle smile. "He died saving my life," he replied, looking down at the roses. "Some flowers are the least I can do for him."

"I hope I'm not intruding." She was dressed all in black, and her gold cross was hanging around her neck as always. She placed a small bouquet of daisies next to the roses. She smiled at the grave. "He's with the angels now."

His eyes filled with tears. "I was so awful to him, for so long, and he still—" His voice choked up, and he couldn't continue.

"You tried to atone at the end, Eric." She took a deep breath. "I told you—you've always been a good person—you just didn't think sometimes, is all. That doesn't make you a bad person." She smiled. "Sean wouldn't have given his life for yours if he didn't think yours had value."

Eric closed his eyes, and in his mind he saw three boys running through the woods behind his house, playing Pirates. Sean always came up with the best games. They were never bored when he was around. He loved to tell stories and could make up great ones on the spur of the moment right off the top of his head. He saw Sean stumble over a tree root, turn a complete somersault, and land on his butt with a big grin on his face. He threw his head back and his joyful laugh echoed through the trees. Eric opened his eyes. "That does help some," he said quietly.

"And your gift?"

He didn't ask how she knew about that. She just seemed to

have a way of knowing things, and sometimes it was better not to ask questions. "It's going away. I talked to this doctor, and he seemed to think when my memory came back—" He paused. "The way he explained it to me was it was like my brain flipped a switch and my memory was gone—and at the same time flipped a switch that let me see into people's minds. When the memory switch flipped back, the other flipped off."

"Or once Coach Walton was gone and the truth was out, God decided you didn't need it anymore." She gave him a knowing smile. "Did it help you?"

"It helped some," he admitted.

"Then that's all that matters, isn't it?"

"I guess," he replied, thinking, *She's really pretty when she smiles.*

"So, what's next for you?" she asked.

"We've got another dozen roses for Paul Benson's grave. We're going to drive over to Oakhurst." He lowered his voice. "I still don't feel right about my part in that."

"He's in a better place now, and his suffering is over." She looked up at the sky. "Ask his forgiveness. I'm sure he'll give it to you. But you also need to forgive yourself, Eric." She winked at him. "Just keep being a good person. That way you'll honor them both." She walked away.

Eric watched her go. The breeze rustled through the trees. He looked up at the sky. There were some dark clouds coming in from the west, and the air was starting to get damp. *Better get back to the car before it starts to rain*, he thought.

"Good-bye, Sean," he said out loud. "I'm sorry again for everything, and thank you. I don't know how else to thank you. But I think trying to be a better person, trying to be more like you, is the way to go."

He managed to get himself turned around. He had just swung

the crutches forward and was about to move his legs when a hand grasped his shoulder.

He froze.

He heard the sound of Sean's laughter from behind him, and he felt it wrap itself around him.

He felt peace.

And then, it faded away into the wind.

He slowly turned his head.

There was no one there.

He smiled and headed for the car.

About the Author

GREG HERREN is the award-winning author of fourteen novels, and has edited eight anthologies, including the award-winning *Love Bourbon Street: Reflections On New Orleans*. He currently lives in New Orleans. He has published over fifty short stories and is a member of the Mystery Writers of America, the International Association of Crime Writers, Private Eye Writers of America, and Sisters in Crime. He has worked as a personal trainer and published over fifty articles on health and fitness. He began his career as a book reviewer and has published over a thousand reviews and interviews with authors as varied as Margaret Cho, Dorothy Allison, and Laura Lippman. A longtime resident of New Orleans, the flavor and culture of his beloved adopted city colors all of his work.

Books Available From Bold Strokes Books

Sleeping Angel by Greg Herren. Eric Matthews survives a terrible car accident only to find out everyone in town thinks he's a murderer—and he has to clear his name even though he has no memories of what happened. (978-1-60282-214-6)

Mesmerized by David-Matthew Barnes. Through her close friendship with Brodie and Lance, Serena Albright learns about the many forms of love and finds comfort for the grief and guilt she feels over the brutal death of her older brother, the victim of a hate crime. (978-1-60282-191-0)

The Perfect Family by Kathryn Shay. A mother and her gay son stand hand in hand as the storms of change engulf their perfect family and the life they knew. (978-1-60282-181-1)

Father Knows Best by Lynda Sandoval. High school juniors and best friends Lila Moreno, Meryl Morganstern, and Caressa Thibodoux plan to make the most of the summer before senior year. What they discover that amazing summer about girl power, growing up, and trusting friends and family more than prepares them to tackle that all-important senior year! (978-1-60282-147-7)